Days & Nights

Stories of classic Japanese women's literature

Hayashi Fumiko

Translated by J.D. Wisgo

Published by Arigatai Books

For questions or comments about this book, please contact the publisher via arigataibooks@gmail.com

Please see https://www.arigataibooks.com for more information on our books.

Edition: 1.0b

ISBN: 978-1-7373182-0-0

CONTENTS

ACKNOWLEDGMENTS

I'd like to thank my wife for all her support on this project. I would also like to thank Kaimai Mizuhiro and Takamasa Kuribayashi for helping confirm the meaning of the original Japanese text in a few places. Finally, I would like to thank Jim Miles and M. McCarn for proofreading assistance.

TRANSLATOR'S INTRODUCTION

When I first read a few of Hayashi Fumiko's stories, I was drawn in by the true-to-life expression of her characters' emotions and the situations she places them in. Then when I discovered that many of her stories had not been translated to English, I knew that this was an excellent opportunity to introduce the stories of a great author to a wider audience.

With our e-books of Hayashi Fumiko's stories, one common request was for a paperback edition. That's why it was an easy decision to use these stories for Arigatai Books' first paperback book. Besides all the stories from "Days & Nights" and "Downfall and Other Stories," I've translated and included another story specially for this release, "The Tryst," where Hayashi Fumiko gives her unique treatment of a complex relationship.

"Days and Nights" is not only the title of one of the stories but also alludes to a theme running through many of these works: long term human relationships that span across months, if not years. Often, those whom we spend our days and nights with we would consider family, at least in some form.

I hope you enjoy the stories!

—J.D. Wisgo

ABOUT CURRENCIES AND EXCHANGE RATES

The term "sen" that appears in this book is an older form of Japanese currency that once represented 1/100th of a yen, issued in both coin and banknote form. Having been removed from circulation in 1953, it is no longer used in modern times.

The stories in this collection were written in the 1930s and 1940s. In 1940, one US dollar was roughly equivalent to 4.27 yen or 427 sen. For comparison, at the time of this book's first publishing (June 2021), the exchange rate was around 109 yen to a single US dollar.

It also should be noted that there were major fluctuations between the yen and the US dollar in the 1940s, so getting an accurate conversion can be difficult.

THE MASTER OF THE WANDERER'S TAVERN

It was a chilly, sand-blown day, and a station attendant was splashing water onto the train platform. Leaning on the wall of a windowless waiting room, Takayoshi stared vacantly at the passing electric and steam trains.

The tips of his toes hurt. The sky looked as if something cold was about to rain down, and the electronic clock hanging down from the center of the platform showed a little past four as darkness drifted through the air of the bustling station. Young people, brimming with self-confidence, haven't the slightest fear of unfinished business, but once you reach age fifty the unfinished becomes the ultimate source of anxiety, a vacuum bereft of even the slightest value. Absorbed in these complex, difficult-to-express feelings, Takayoshi lit his pipe and decided to take the long way home.

About a month earlier he had withdrawn from Manchuria, bringing Taeko with him. He had no living relatives in Japan, but after returning to his hometown Takayoshi was glad he did. There was a cozy, comfortable feeling, like when you put your arms through an old lined kimono. His wife had been born in a city in Kōshū called Kajikazawa, but because she came to Tokyo as a child she didn't even know how to properly write "Kajikazawa."

Twenty-five years ago he married Itoko, at that time working as a nurse in a Tokyo hospital, and they soon crossed over to Manchuria, starting in Fengtian and moving on to a variety of places until the end of the war, heading even as far as the Northern tip of Manchuria. They lived in Hailar for around four years. There they ran a high-end grocery store near the station with their three daughters, the oldest being twenty, but his wife and second oldest daughter died of tuberculosis right as the war ended, and the oldest went missing in Hsinking, leaving only Takayoshi and his youngest daughter. Taeko was seventeen, and had never stepped foot in Japan.

One of his friends that had shared the same joys and sorrows on the ship home was a man by the name of Ryōtarō Kawabe, an employee of the South Manchuria Railway the same age as Takayoshi. Because he had left his family in Tokyo, Ryōtarō had no problems finding a place to live when he returned. His family even had an estate of nearly a half-acre near Toyamagahara, where a house stood that had escaped from the fires of war. Initially Takayoshi stayed in Ryōtarō's house. He had no money or possessions but was a simple man, an optimist at heart, and his ability to remain calm in any environment was undoubtedly a result of the selflessness and indifference to material objects gained from wandering the continent at length. Ryōtarō's wife was a teacher for home economics in a private girls' college, but she didn't receive her husband's troublesome traveling companion well.

Taeko had the consideration to keep her mother's keepsake, a diamond ring, hidden in an inside pocket of her pants. Hair trimmed short, she hid her mother's platinum watch in one ear and her gold ring in another, behind an old, dirty bandage wrapped from the top of her head to her chin, as if suffering from two ear infections.

Takayoshi was completely unaware of this and thought that she truly had a problem with her ears. The bandage was dirtied in places by blood smears. The gaunt, haggard form of this tall seventeen-year-old, only a shadow of her former self, didn't catch anyone's attention.

Kept safe by his daughter's body, these three treasures returned unharmed to their former country. Of his daughters, Taeko had the most attractive features, and about a month after returning to Japan her beauty began to shine remarkably. She had an extremely open-minded nature. At the boarding house of the lady's college in Hsinking, Taeko was given the nickname "poison girl" because she possessed a hidden power to manipulate any of the teachers as she pleased. Because of her height and dark skin, she looked a year or two older than her age. When she smiled, her savagely beautiful set of white teeth bestowed her an amazing charm, and despite having eyes and thick eyebrows that were close together, her large eyes glowed with an inner passion.

Her slender neck appeared delicate, but she had a beautifully pure voice. Coming to Japan for the first time in her life, it seemed as if her motherland had actually provided ample comfort to heal all of her sufferings, even the memories of countless days of hardship during their escape home.

As the days passed even Takayoshi, who had lost his wife, his daughters, and all of his possessions, managed to obtain a sort of resignation, and made sixty thousand yen by selling some trifling jewelry that Taeko had brought with them. With the help of Ryōtarō he obtained some cheap goods from a small market in the Ikebukuro shopping district where he opened a tiny bar. He gave the bar the tongue-in-cheek name "The Wanderer's Tavern" and worked there ardently with Taeko. Business was exceptionally well, perhaps due to the timing of their opening, and they had a relatively strong customer base, with Takayoshi's careful saké selection leading to a gradual increase of regular customers. Among them were customers who came seeking Taeko, but she was well aware of such clientele and dealt with them tactfully.

Despite the bar's success, Takayoshi didn't truly enjoy himself; even though he worked very hard Takayoshi lacked both the ambition and desire of his early years. His sole enjoyment came from making small talk over drinks with his saké-loving friend Ryōtarō in a tiny back room.

The dirt floor inside the bar was only around ten meters square with a dreary atmosphere consisting of a couple of shabby tables and chairs, the paper-covered ceiling dirtied by a collection of spots from rain leaks. The back room was around ten by three meters, a dull place with an army blanket spread over the damaged tatami mats, and a small electric heated table. The kitchen took up around five square meters of the dirt floor and was the only place where an abundance of saké and stocked foodstuffs were tightly packed. At the exit to the kitchen they kept two white Leghorn roosters in a box that was hand made by Takayoshi. Being an early waker, he kept the roosters simply because he liked to hear them crow.

Even in Manchuria, Takayoshi had raised many roosters. Hearing the shameless crowing of the roosters in the faint light of dawn brought back memories. He got a special feeling whenever he mused about the past as he smoked lying stomach-down on his futon, listening carefully to the voices of the roosters intermittently announcing the time. Sleeping soundly beside him, there was something in Taeko's features that closely resembled his deceased wife, making him recall a tender memory from his early days with her…When he thought how even the trip leaving Japan with his young wife, almost like they were eloping, had been reduced to a mere fragment of a memory, and how the woman who had been at his side through thick and thin was now in the world of the dead and not with him, a frigid desolation overwhelmed his body. It sounds funny to say, but he truly felt that a wife was a nice thing to have. As he aged, his numerous friends left one at a time, and in the present time, when even a certain woman he had unchaste intentions for had disappeared into a world of mist, his late wife was all he could remember.

As he listened to the roosters crowing, Takayoshi fondly recollected the pleasant days when would talk with his wife until dawn, their warm bodies close. Even during the years he was married, when he went on business trips to various places Takayoshi had spent time with a handful of women on the spur of the moment, but now all he could recall were empty faces, blank like rice paddles. Lying beside his daughter, a part of his beloved wife, Takayoshi felt a warm happiness, knowing that no woman could surpass his wife.

He didn't know what sort of man his daughter would end up with, but he hoped that she would choose a good man and lead a happy life. Her hair had an unpleasant smell, apparently not having been washed for some time, and her lips slightly parted below a well-formed nose strongly resembled Itoko. Taeko looked peaceful as she slept, the deep shadow cast by her eyelashes giving her a genuine charm.

Gazing at his daughter's sleeping form, Takayoshi began sinking into a loneliness that made him sob like a little boy. He felt that family was far more precious than wealth or possessions. Strange things ran through his mind, like his deceased wife returning to him in the form of a ghost. Perhaps due to his age, life seemed terribly empty, and as he listened to the roosters each morning Takayoshi would daydream about those days that were the prime of his life.

The wind blows through my house
My bed, bitter cold throughout the night
I see how the weather and the seasons have changed
Sleepless, I come to know the true length of the night

Takayoshi liked this passage from some poem—capturing feelings that would emerge from somewhere deep inside him, making him yearn to be with someone else, especially in the mornings when the pale moon was out. Sometimes Ryōtarō would half-jokingly say to him, "It sure is lonely without many good friends around. I know a widow who is about to turn 38, would you be interested? Do you have any desire to get married again?" Takayoshi would answer, "I don't want to get married this late in my life and go through all that trouble for nothing," although he still felt young at heart. It wasn't like he didn't want anything to do with women. At times he had an aching need for a woman, but as he watched Taeko gradually grow up, he also understood that it was time to abandon the crude desires of a man.

He questioned the purpose of getting another wife now and

spending a few more years living a boring, repetitive life, and yet in the entire five years since Itoko fell ill and passed away, Takayoshi had lived his days devoutly like a priest. Fortunately, he was able to keep himself busy due to the continuing war, and as a result never experienced the true misery of a living, breathing man. If there was ever even a hint of such a thing, he would drown his sorrows in saké.

But when the war ended Takayoshi's fate suddenly changed, and he fell into the squalor of living in a shack-like barracks that bore no resemblance to what it once had been.

In the present, after his life had been changed drastically as if sliced in two by a great blade, all thought was pointless. But he also felt that saké would be no match for a flesh-and-blood person, and it would be wrong to say there weren't times when his crude desires would spark up, a yearning for an old man's final blaze. The roosters crowed bravely each morning, announcing the hour. Whenever Takayoshi heard their voices he became absorbed in the same thoughts, letting out a succession of sighs that doubled as yawns.

Then one day, Ryōtarō brought in the widow. She was an unexpectedly youthful woman, short but a little chubby, with a round face that was not quite beautiful yet possessed a certain charm, and a personality that was not somber like you would expect from a widow. Ryōtarō said her husband, a combat medic first lieutenant, had died in battle in Manila and she had no children, managing to make a living with dressmaking. Larger, taller women were what Takayoshi preferred, and this woman was the opposite of that, yet there was something very likable about her appearance. Even her hands were beautiful. Unlike his deceased wife the widow was fair-skinned, and in her soft, yet passionate eyes Takayoshi could sense a certain kindness. Taeko acted nonchalant, but Takayoshi could tell that she understood because she seemed to try and curry favor with the widow by requesting for a dress to be sewn. Taeko was skilled at tactfully using others and seemed to be already taking into account preparations for the coming cold weather.

The arranged meeting was a casual affair, and however you look at it these two were strangers to one another. But even if they were to get married, sleeping together in a tiny room, in the same bed with an adolescent daughter was no way to get rid of the awkwardness of strangers. Taeko was an incorrigible, strong-willed woman. Takayoshi was forced to think hard about what to do. According to what Ryōtarō said a few days later, if the woman Hana Miyauchi had feelings for Takayoshi, then at least his interest should have been piqued. As a man in his 50s who had completely given up on himself, Takayoshi was somewhat pleased just to have been found attractive by a younger woman.

"It turns out that Ms. Miyauchi previously worked at the same lady's college where my wife was employed. Ms. Miyauchi is used to dealing with younger women, so she's also made a good impression with Taeko. She's really excited to make some winter clothes for her."

Takayoshi had a good feeling about this.

He was told that Hana was born in Shinano Province and with only a single living relative, her younger sister, she was currently staying with the family of a friend. Hana was at the point where she would have to move out as soon as she found a husband, but even if she were to move, there was the matter of her two sewing machines and a few other personal belongings, which is why there was no way Takayoshi would let her stay at his barracks-like house.

Ryōtarō made a suggestion. "This is a rare opportunity. You should find a suitable room around here and move in with Hana. I'm sure you can leave Taeko where she is now, keeping watch over the bar."

"That's not going to work. After all, Taeko is still a child, and it would be dangerous to leave her alone like that."

Ryōtarō laughed. "Taeko can handle herself better than you. She's a clever girl and can get by fine on her own. If you want, I can talk to her myself."

His manner suggested he was trying to settle this matter as soon as possible.

Takayoshi struggled to decide. Having been through many hardships with Taeko, he felt it would be cruel to only consider his own happiness. But Taeko was cheerful as ever, and never broached the topic of Hana with him.

Less than ten days later after they met, Taeko received a gray suit and pink blouse from Hana. The material for the suit had been selected and purchased by Takayoshi at the same market for a relatively inexpensive price. The pink crepe blouse was prepared specially by Hana, which pleased Takayoshi even more than Taeko, and seeing Hana's truly kind gesture of waiving her sewing fee motivated him to quickly move the marriage arrangement forward.

Then one night before bed, Takayoshi casually broached the topic of Hana. "About that arrangement by Ryōtarō…" Taeko looked at her father briefly with a serious expression, but the next moment a faint smile surfaced on her lips.

"I'm fine with anything that will make you happy, Dad. But I don't want to take care of the bar here all by myself…I wonder if I would be able to commute here from somewhere else…"

"Commute…from where?"

"You see, I've found a nice place. Recently I've been wanting to go there, but I've kept quiet about it since I thought you would get upset…"

Hearing this from his daughter, Takayoshi didn't know what to say. Being casually told about a "nice place" made him begin to recall the faces of the customers that came to see Taeko.

"It's not him, or him either…" thought Takayoshi as he went through each of the regular customers. Who in the world could she be talking about? Something didn't sit right with him, as if a wrongdoing had been committed.

"I guess maybe you met someone at school."

Staring at the ceiling, Takayoshi purposefully suggested something unlikely. A rat was running around somewhere, making a lot of noise. There was an extraordinary number of rats in this area, boldly appearing in places like the kitchen, even in broad daylight.

"No, it's not a woman. It's a man."

"Oh..." Takayoshi groaned.

He had the feeling that the daughter he still considered a child had suddenly become a full-grown adult.

"Who is it? Someone from the bar?"

"He only came to the bar once. It's a person from Manchuria...someone I met on the road..."

"Someone you met only once or twice is asking you to come and live with him?"

"Goodness no, I've seen him countless times. We even met yesterday."

Now that she mentioned it, there were indeed many times when she would go out somewhere and disappear for a while. It wasn't for long enough to affect business so Takayoshi hadn't minded, but those times she must have been secretly meeting with a man, he realized, and made a deep groaning sound in his chest.

"At your age, I think that's still a tad early. I don't know what kind of person he is, but I doubt if it's a good idea to go through all the trouble of starting a family this early. Above all, it's a huge financial burden. But everyone has dreams when they are young. I'm not going to tell you how to live your life, but I'm saying this because, as your father, I'm worried about you."

Taeko rolled around onto her belly, propping herself on her elbows.

"I'll be fine. Just pretend I died in Manchuria. Because it's going to be really hard for you to find a room here. Even if you are just renting a small room, you'll need tens of thousands of yen for a down payment. Have her come stay here, and I'll move out and commute here for work. Just give me a monthly salary. If you would only do that, I'd be really happy..."

Still staring at the roof, Takayoshi was speechless. Taeko had a vacant look and seemed to be thinking about something, but she eventually started whistling.

"What does this guy do for a living?" he asked.

"Newspaper reporter. He's started to make a name for himself around Hsinking. He had a wife and a child, but the wife passed away, and the child is being raised by relatives, leaving him to an apartment alone. It's really close by...He says he's 35...but he looks really young. There's something about him that reminds me of you when you were young, Dad."

Takayoshi closed his eyes, amused. Yes, she was his daughter, but she was also a respectable woman. Even at his age, he was embarrassed to ask Taeko about how far they had taken their relationship, but if she was considering moving in then things must be pretty serious. She was right, Takayoshi could simply pretend she died, he thought painfully. He couldn't help but call to mind all the hardships they had for over a year in Manchuria.

"In the beginning, he was a man with a sharp tongue, easily angered. But now I see he is a gentle person. He even spoke highly of you. He is very kind, and lately has been doing whatever I ask of him."

Well, well...Takayoshi opened his eyes again and looked at the ceiling. It was said that a young woman held in store surprising things and so must be handled with care...and Takayoshi found amusement in this world of humans, where the right season triggers changes in a woman to attract a mate—like pollen being released to attract bees. Perhaps it was better to end this stupidity of working only with his daughter, at times reminiscing about the past or lamenting the world together. It was no surprise that Taeko wanted to break off this lonesome relationship with her father and start considering building her own foundation and her own future, the way she liked. Takayoshi suddenly thought of Hana's narrow eyes.

"Your ages are pretty far apart."

"Yeah, sometimes he laughs about how we are like the 'Ohan Chōemon'...I have no idea what that means, nor do I care. Because we are happy together...Sometimes we don't have enough to eat, but that doesn't bother either of us. That's why if you can give me a monthly salary, I'll be able to move there and continue working at the restaurant, bringing loads of drinks for everyone and making a great deal of money for you at The Wanderer's Tavern…and Dad, you'll be happy too if you just marry Ms. Miyauchi. You won't need to listen to the roosters anymore since she will comfort you, right?"

Taeko giggled. She hadn't forgotten Takayoshi's habit of saying that hearing the roosters reminded him of her mother.

A few days later, Taeko gathered up her meager personal belongings and headed to Iori's apartment with Takayoshi. They arrived to find Iori waiting in his freshly cleaned room. Taeko was unusually dressed up, wearing the gray suit sewn by Hana. She looked twenty years of age, perhaps due to her large frame. Her waist bulged out a little, and the silk socks Takayoshi had specially bought for her made her legs look slender, like a western girl. Her sandals, with red velvet soles, gave her an alluring appeal.

Iori was a surprisingly youthful man, remarkably tall with a wonderfully wide, fair-skinned forehead. But most imposing was his bulky, well-formed physique. Iori was a good complement for the large-bodied Taeko, and Takayoshi was secretly pleased with how well-matched of a couple they were.

He thought this was a nice man indeed. Iori's physique was very different than the weak-looking guys he saw around town, and there was a trustworthy quality to him. Furthermore, unlike a man in his twenties Iori was extremely calm—as was to be expected from someone who had a child and was once married—spoke rationally, and had excellent common sense. To Takayoshi's surprise, the tiny dresser Taeko had been using every day was already arranged next to the window.

Taeko quickly went out to get some beef and vegetables, and cooked sukiyaki for them. Every little thing there reminded Takayoshi of when he first got married. It was as if his early days with Itoko, when she had been working as a nurse, were being reenacted here. Takayoshi drank heavily, content to have encountered the kindness of these young people. He learned that Iori's young girl was going to be six, and his wife, a woman from Iori's hometown, had passed away from lung disease. Feeling a strong empathy because his wife suffered from the same ailment, Takayoshi was surprised to see how two couples could be so alike. Iori also drank a good amount, and said he was embarrassed about hiding his relationship with Taeko.

Iori was receiving a salary of 2,700 yen but had to send 500 yen each month to support his child, so he asked Takayoshi to please be understanding of this. Takayoshi felt his eyes begin to tear up. Such honesty was a rare thing.

As soon as Takayoshi returned home, leaving Taeko at Iori's apartment, he contacted Ryōtarō and conveyed his intent to proceed with the marriage arrangement. As there was an open area behind the back door, he started work there on a space of roughly five meters square. He planned on fitting her two sewing machines and other belongings in that space. Takayoshi obtained permission to build an extension, found a carpenter, and began tearing down a wall. But there was no response from Ryōtarō, even after a few days.

Taeko cheerfully commuted to The Wanderer's Tavern each evening.

"Dad, what's with the fancy clothes all of a sudden?" Taeko teased him.

He wasn't particularly bothered by it, but the lack of a response from Ryōtarō did make him vaguely uneasy. Takayoshi wasn't comfortable with going out there himself, so he tried sending Taeko to Ryōtarō's place on an errand. When Taeko returned around nighttime, she didn't look very happy.

"Dad, Ms. Miyauchi isn't going to work out. She's a very odd woman…I heard that she was in love with a younger man, and suddenly left for Yokosuka without telling anyone…although she isn't with that man…and I changed my mind about you and her getting together. I had thought things were going almost too well, but Mr.

Kawabe said that a woman like that would be more difficult to handle than me. I thought that you marrying such an indecisive person would only lead to misery and that you would probably eventually give up on her yourself, so I went there to ask them to please refuse the offer. Mr. Kawabe said that if he finds another good person he will introduce her, and that he will come by sometime tomorrow."

Takayoshi did not take the news very well. He was committed to marrying Hana, and had been dreaming about their wonderful life together. Takayoshi was even planning on using both roosters at the bar and felt pitiful for having already taken into consideration his new wife's quality of sleep. He had used an expensive type of lumber, but the once-pleasing scent of fresh wood now made Takayoshi uncomfortable.

Takayoshi had come to the Tokyo station today, determined to pay a visit to the Miyauchi residence whose location he heard about from Ryōtarō, but he felt weighted down by the terrible racket produced by countless trains coming and going.

The marriage arrangement that had involved an old man like him was, by pure chance, stuck in an unfinished state, but surely there was no purpose to chasing the woman at this point.

As Takayoshi stood in the station for a while, watching the bustling crowds entering and exiting the trains, an overwhelming loneliness struck him. What a fool I am, he thought, reminded of the play "Sanemori."

Thinking it wouldn't be so bad to live out the rest of his life as the owner of The Wanderer's Tavern, Takayoshi casually looked around the station. Even in a place like this without any greenery, a hint of the chilly November weather hung in the air.

Each person getting on or off a train had a life to live. Takayoshi himself would most likely hear the voices of the roosters again tomorrow as they heralded the coming of morning. And that wasn't altogether a bad thing.

It is in our nature as humans, and will always be, to suffer from these chance events and be driven into hopeless situations, thought Takayoshi as he realized how miserable his life of fifty years had become, stepping firmly on his chilly toes as he walked down towards one of the train platforms.

DOWNFALL

I went off to Tokyo without my family's permission. Shortly after the war ended, the people from Tokyo who had evacuated to my village rushed home. Despite everyone having said they would spend the rest of their lives in the countryside, the moment the war ended they all went back to Tokyo, including Mr. Honda and Mr. Sanro. I wanted to go see Tokyo for myself, curious about whether it was really such a great place. My older sister had spent a long time working as a live-in maid, but once the war began she returned home to help out the family. My younger brothers both enlisted for the war, but being stationed in Japan they returned as soon as the war ended and loafed around at home. My sister said that we'd probably have to find someplace to work soon. We had very little in the way of rice fields, and the older of my brothers said that with all these healthy people crowding under a single roof we were going to soon have trouble making ends meet. As part of a family of eight I had three other younger siblings, so my father got in the habit of saying how just keeping everyone fed was a major headache. I made up my mind and asked a friend working at the train station to buy me a ticket to Tokyo. I packed ten days' worth of food in my backpack so my mother wouldn't find out, and last October came to Tokyo by myself on a night stream train. "When you come to Tokyo, please stop by our house. We'd love to repay your kindness." Mr.

Sanro's wife had said this every time she came to our house to buy rice and vegetables, so as soon as I arrived I found my way to their house. I was wondering how large their residence was because Mr. Sanro said he owned a factory, and even a cottage at someplace called Atami, but it turns out they lived in a surprisingly tiny house. Mr. Sanro's wife stared at me in bewilderment. When I told her that I had run away from home she gave me a worried look and said, "In Tokyo food is very scarce. To begin with, our house was burned down and we ended up having to borrow someone else's." I decided to ask them to let me stay for only two days and immediately began searching for a place to work. A significant portion of Tokyo was destroyed. The city was burned to a shocking degree, and this deeply pained me. Mr. Sanro's wife complained constantly about the countryside, saying all people from the country were bad, which upset me. She was very servile when living in the country, but after returning to Tokyo had a change of heart to the point where she even wanted the clock and clothes returned that she bartered for rice. Mr. Sanro's wife gave me two of her daughter's items of clothing, but she complained so much that I wanted to return them. I don't believe Mr. Sanro's family are good people. Besides the wife, there was the husband's mother and two daughters who were attending a women's college. Everyone was so snooty, and when I went to sleep they gave me the dirtiest, most ragged futon they had. I stayed at Mr. Sanro's house for only one evening and then headed to Ueno station. That's when I met Koyama. As I was standing idly, waiting to get on a train at Ueno station, a man suddenly asked me, "Hey, where are you off to?" I told him that I had come to Tokyo in search of work and asked an acquaintance for help, but because I was treated so badly I was going to return to the country—except that I couldn't afford to buy a ticket home. The man then said that if I wanted to work in Tokyo, he would find me whatever job I wanted, so I should come to stay in his boarding house. Being desperate I didn't care where I stayed, and I went with him. The man lived in an apartment in a place called Urawa. It was a decrepit, utterly miserable second-floor apartment, and in the tiny, seven-square-meter room was nothing but a futon and a few cooking utensils. The insides of the heavily worn tatami mat were exposed, and the grimy futon beside the window looked as if it hadn't been cleaned in months. Koyama was employed at a small pharmaceutical company in Kanda. He was in his forties. I couldn't figure out why he was so wealthy.

Koyama told me his wife was killed in the air raids, and now he lives alone. That night, I slept together with Koyama on the same futon. He did some things that at first surprised me, and I couldn't help being afraid of, but when I thought about going back home to the country I was able to endure it all. Koyama said he thought I was already a woman in my twenties. When I told him I was still eighteen, he remarked how country girls look mature. But I didn't let that bother me. Thinking about things doesn't change anything, so I was just happy there was someone who treated me this kindly. Koyama was extremely good to me. I started gradually becoming attracted to him too. After he came home from work, we would go out to see a movie. Before long, the cold winter came around. As I had no warm clothes, I told Koyama I was considering going home to the country to pick some up. But he said I mustn't go home, and managed to gather a few clothes for me from somewhere, including a warm coat. I went downtown by myself and got a perm at a beauty salon. Koyama said I was so stylish that I looked like a western woman. He also said that if I was a dancer I'd probably be a big hit. I went and bought a newspaper and tried searching for jobs like that, but I thought that Koyama wouldn't approve so I applied to one in secret. The job was at a dance hall that catered to Japanese customers, and inexperienced applicants were required to attend training for two weeks. I visited every day from morning to evening. That's where I met Kuriyama, who said he was a musician. He had just been discharged from the army, and was a good-natured man with a pure heart. For some reason, I felt comfortable speaking with Kuriyama. He generally ate out using government-issued meal tickets but said he wanted to have a home-cooked meal once in a while, so one day I took him home to my apartment in Urawa. I cooked for Kuriyama the black-market rice Koyama had bought me along with sardines and miso-seasoned meat. When I told him about how I had left my home in the country and was now living with Koyama, he seemed surprised and said, "I find it hard to believe you're such an ignorant woman. When I saw you, I got the impression you were an incredibly smart, clever woman, but I guess God works in strange ways. I guess you're optimistic about the world, but you're living a very dangerous life." However, in this day and age it turns out that many women who live in Tokyo for only a few months end up just like me. When I took Kuriyama to the station I bumped into Koyama carrying a large package wrapped in cloth. Kuriyama quickly left and boarded the train. After returning home to the apartment and being severely scolded by Koyama, he grabbed my hair and gave me a terrible beating. That experience made me instantly detest him and shudder in fear. When I slipped on my coat, intending to leave, Koyama swiftly knocked me down and kicked me several times in the stomach. The pain was excruciating, as if my back would split open. Koyama dragged me to the futon, grabbed a pair of scissors, and cut my permed hair off without a word. For the next two or three days my body ached to the point I could barely move. When I glanced in the mirror, I was happy to see my eyelashes were uncommonly long. My cheekbones were a little high, but when I put on lipstick, my full lips gave the appearance of a western girl. With my large, shiny teeth and larger-than-average breasts, I felt somehow prettier than all the girls who had been to the dance hall a few times. A dance teacher glanced at my legs and complimented me on how nice they were. I was even taller than all the women who applied to the job opening. I'll never forget the many gorgeous sights at that bar. But sleeping on a dirty futon, sharing a pillow with an older man in a dirty apartment—I was utterly fed up with this lifestyle. Kuriyama had said God had made me in a strange way, but I couldn't bear to stay in a place like this. Whenever I thought deeply about things, a terribly unpleasant feeling surged through my body. I didn't want to think anymore. In a few days I left that place. I knew where a woman lived who ran an oden hot pot stall in front of the station, so I went there. She had two children and lived in a house behind a car garage. The woman gladly let me stay with her, having known me from frequenting her stall. Well, it is said that this world is filled with kindness, but in any case I continued commuting from there to the dance hall. Around that time, Kuriyama began working at a different establishment. When I went to visit him there, he said, "I know I'm probably being unreasonable, but I'm a selfish, scrupulous man, and I don't enjoy being with you." These days, Kuriyama was a man pursuing only idealistic, unobtainable things. Hearing that he didn't enjoy being with me actually seemed to encourage me. I hadn't seen Kuriyama in two full months. But despite that, the more time that went by without seeing him, the more I couldn't help constantly thinking about him. I hadn't seen Koyama in a very long time, nor did I consider going to see him. A few times I went to stay at an inn in the country with another man, and recently I've been getting the feeling that I've become a bad woman; at times it even seemed like a frigid wind blew right through my soul. Even the woman I was living with said that lately my appearance has changed drastically. Her house was a gloomy, cramped place with only a pair of ten-square-meter rooms, but I grew to love it. The woman had a fourteen-year-old daughter and a twelve-year-old son, and I was surprised to see they were both such good-mannered children, spoke properly like members of a well-to-do family, and always listened to their mother. No matter how late I came home, the woman would never complain, and she treated me like one of her own children, making me feel it was very rare to find someone with such a kind heart.

I met a certain office worker at the dance hall. It was a man who never danced, not even a little. He always arrived with a companion and idly watched other people dance. One day, I happened to run across him at the Yaesu exit of the station, and he treated me to tea as we chatted for a while. He told me he was recently decommissioned from the army after a stay in Java and hadn't found a job yet. Upon returning, he found his wife with another man, his house destroyed by fire, and he was now staying with a friend. "There's nothing particularly interesting in this world but nothing bad either. I live my days relying only on chance," he said. "I don't consider myself a very bright person," he continued. "But having been forsaken by my own life long ago, each day is like a terrible hangover." I was feeling lonely, so I became attracted to this man Seki. He was tall, skinny, and had a bluish-black complexion. Seki had a habit of asking, "What's up? Anything interesting going on?" each time we met. And I would always respond, "Yes, despite it all, things are interesting." When summer rolled in, we went to the Ōhito Hot Springs in Izu together. We stayed in a traditional inn. Seki brought whiskey, and I brought some rice I had my aunt buy for me. It was an ordinary inn in the middle of a field, and we drank whiskey until late at night, listening to the voices of the frogs outside. Seki talked constantly about dying. I talked constantly about how living was more interesting. Perhaps because of the alcohol, after he went inside the mosquito net Seki fell silent and began to cry. I couldn't help but find his behavior strange. In the middle of the night, I went into a hot spring by myself. We returned to Tokyo after staying in Ōhito for a single night. A few days later, Seki committed suicide. By that time I guess he was already knocking on death's door. I was depressed for a few days, but I gradually forgot about Seki. I changed jobs to another dance hall, using the alias "Momo." Every day I was preoccupied, busy with only dancing and enjoying myself, and there was no time to even think about my hometown or my future. I used up all of my money and was poor as usual, but whenever I wanted to eat something a stranger would treat me to a meal.

In September, I realized that there was something different about my body. I immediately thought of Seki, but didn't want to give birth to a child. When I talked to the woman I was staying with, she said I had to have the baby, no matter what. She said that once I did, even a girl like me would surely mature and start thinking about the future.

But I didn't want to think at all about having a child. I danced at the hall for hours on end without stopping for rest. I pitied any baby who would be born from a woman like me. Soon, the autumn winds began to blow. I bumped into Koyama on a street in Shinjuku. He was a total wreck. It seemed his life hadn't gone very well since we'd parted ways. We stood and talked for a little while, when he said, "I went through hell for you," and told me how he was at the police station for two months.

Koyama said he would pull himself together and asked if we could try to make things work again, but I flatly refused. He stared at me dumbfoundedly, saying how this country girl was now a completely different person, transformed into a young lady. When Koyama asked what I was doing lately, I lied to him and said I was a movie actress. When I told him I would probably become an assistant for a famous actress in the next year or two, he suddenly turned serious and began to plead, "I promise to not do anything to you anymore, so would you consider living with me?" I could barely contain my laughter. I thought that all men were such weak things. I detested weak men. Koyama invited me to get some tea, but I told him I was headed to work and quickly left, thinking he probably didn't have enough money to even afford tea. There is no way I'd ever fall in love with a man like Koyama. When I entered Shinjuku station, I suddenly realized a pretty woman was standing beside me. With a gray suit, a large brown handbag and shoes of the same color, her makeup-less face had beautiful smooth skin, kept in perfect condition through daily care, and her eyes seemed to sparkle. The men who happened to pass by all took notice of her, turning to me and smiling awkwardly, making me feel like I was being made a fool of. But when I went to the dance hall and looked around at my coworkers, I couldn't find a single beautiful woman like the young lady I saw at Shinjuku station. Unlike us, that girl must have been from a very wealthy family. When I stared into the mirror, I got the feeling that I was somehow different from the proper women of society. Us girls at the dance hall have developed a unique style of makeup to make us stand out from the others. We surrounded our eyes with dark ink and covered our lips with deep red lipstick. Because it was hard to find good cream these days, some girls even put cooking oil on their back and legs, but the stink of tempura displeased customers. I wore cellophane-like, semi-transparent clothes that made me feel like the circus woman who had come to the country once a long time ago. Ever since seeing that woman at the station, I have felt somehow dirty and miserable. I wore a glass necklace, a gold-plated bracelet shaped like a snake swallowing its own tail, and a pink, paper-thin dress. In my hair was a large, light blue ribbon, in my ears tiny blue beads, and on my finger a ruby ring. My shoes were a pair of black leather high heels that I barely managed to purchase second-hand with the help of my friend Rose. A man once called me, "The first show horse of the year," and while I didn't know what that meant at the time, when I later found out it really upset me. Kuriyama often used to tell me, "You look much better without any makeup. You've got a large build, so makeup makes you look aged." But I couldn't bear not wearing thick makeup. At the dance hall where I used to work, my manager called me "parakeet girl."

I've been feeling increasingly unwell to the point of wanting to take off work lately. On the days when I didn't work, I slept in bed all day without eating a thing. Concerned for me, the woman living with me cooked something for me to eat, but I didn't have any appetite. I recently took up smoking. Despite feeling I was gradually becoming a terrible woman, I just wasn't able to change my ways. Whenever I got deep in thought, a great sense of hopelessness came over me, so I slept all day, and when I got bored at night I played cards by myself. Whenever I tried to use the cards to read my own fortune, I got the sense that something good was about to happen to me. I felt like I was going to have a beautiful wedding. In a house where sunlight streamed in from all the windows, I would give birth to a cute baby. But as I was thinking about these things, the sound of the dance hall's music suddenly popped into my head again. Even the friends of my coworkers spent their days deceiving and being deceived by men in that dance hall, but the girls, by and large, were mostly on the deceived side—a bunch of surprisingly pure, good-natured girls. Lately, there's been someone coming to the hall who likes me. I don't know what business he is in, but I don't like him because of his snobbish attitude. I find it repulsive how he's always wiping his face with a blue handkerchief, or fixing his hair with a tiny red comb. Strange men of the kind I've never seen back home frequently show up in the hall. I don't have the slightest idea how they make a living. All of my friends have people they like or are dating, but they're infatuated with the type of men who you glance at and think, "who is that guy?" They spend their meaningless days breaking up, finding a new partner, and then repeating the cycle of chance. When night falls, us girls who are, by day, like dreary weeds growing in the shade, finally come around. In the dressing room, there are even girls who take hormones like they are candy. The only things our wrapping cloths contain are dirty slips, pieces of homemade bread, half-sewn blouses, and partially read dirty novels or magazines. Very few of us have any significant amount of money in our handbags. Us show horses are all poor.

Lately, there have been times that I considered going home, but it doesn't go beyond a mere thought; it's not like I'm yearning to return to my hometown so badly that it brings tears. I pay the woman I'm living with 300 yen a month. The woman, with her ever-present kindness, tells me to not work too hard, and that I should eventually find an honest job. But I never graduated high school, so I think I'll never be able to find anything like an honest job. Everyone is saying an age of terrible unemployment is coming. One day, when I stopped by Ginza for the first time in a while, Kuriyama spoke to me with a surprising degree of consideration. "Wherever you go, everything is the same. The fact that the world is filled with women just like you doesn't change anything. Once in a while I worry about what happened to you. But I guess for the time being there's nothing either of us can do." Hearing this touched something deep inside of me. Neither of us was in the mood to drink tea, so we walked the evening streets towards Marunouchi and took a stroll around the Imperial Palace. Insects were buzzing all around, and the feeling of late autumn was in the air. Kuriyama told me he joined a small band and had been touring all over without a break. I thought the scenery on his trip must have been nice, but he said there were many relatives he had to support which made things difficult. When I told him I wanted to get married someday, his expression turned serious and he said, "You think you can get married in this world? Even if you consider marriage, you'll never find a good person." Then I told him that I was probably pregnant, and Kuriyama said, "It's fine, no big deal. You should have the baby. Let me know when it's born, OK? I'll set aside some money for you." Blown by the wind, we walked along the wide streets of the palace grounds. When we parted ways at the Sukiya bridge Kuriyama said, "We'll meet again. Call me anytime," and slipped me an attractive business card along with a pair of hundred-yen bills. He was wearing brand-new shoes. I guess business was going well.

THE TALE OF THE SEISHŪKAN GUEST HOUSE

Returning to Tokyo after a long summer break, Tanimura left his guest house on the outskirts of the city and moved to another one that he discovered on a backstreet near a school.

Gone were the days of opening a window in the morning and looking out at an oak forest, or listening to the sound of a piano played by a beautiful girl in the bungalow next door; now when he opened his window in the evening, the dim lights of the city sparkled and the autumn scenery of Tokyo was an utterly refreshing sight for his eyes, filling his chest with great pride in being able to live in such a metropolis.

Perhaps owing to being a son of Negayama Temple, Tanimura was not known to be one who complains about food. However, the long strand of woman's hair in his mussel soup on the first morning in the house was enough to frustrate even the thick-skinned Tanimura.

Lifting up thick glasses used to correct terrible nearsightedness, Tanimura gently plucked the hair out of his soup, chopsticks still in hand as he wondered whether it belonged to the chubby maid or the squint-eyed maid with a face like a dried salmon.

Even though Tanimura was raised in a temple, he studied medicine with great passion. However, because of his interest in surgery, he had an assortment of surgical knives arranged neatly on his bookcase, glittering like trophies.

Cheeks stuffed full of rice, Tanimura carefully pulled out the long strand of hair and gazed at it silently under a microscope. There was a large amount of mineral oil present. A chain of cells flipped over like a caterpillar, as though declaring, "I am from the chubby maid!"
Trying to suppress his disgust, Tanimura gulped down his diluted bancha tea, then hurriedly put on his hat and headed down the wide corridor towards the front door.

At the entrance, the chubby maid happened to be polishing his shoes.

Tanimura assumed this was a result of his gift of a fifty-sen coin to each of the maids when first arriving yesterday, but when he remembered the long strand of hair in his soup anxiety overcame him.

"Good morning, sir. Were you able to sleep well last night?"

"Why do you ask?"

"Well...it seems that people new to this place have difficulty sleeping."

"Oh really? I slept wonderfully."

Concealing mounting feelings of unease, Tanimura slipped on the shoes that the chubby maid had polished for him. A moment later the unpleasant stench of several days of skipped baths wafted from the maid's unkempt, apparently as yet uncombed hair. In a dream-like state, Tanimura nonchalantly held the cloth-wrapped package against his chest as he plucked a single hair from the maid's head.

"Oh my! Surely you jest..."

Face flushed, the maid covered her chest with both hands and ran giggling towards the kitchen before disappearing.

Just as Tanimura was standing there absent-mindedly, still holding the strand of hair he had removed, the landlady came in from the front desk.

"Oh, good morning. Would you mind putting this on the board with the other nameplates? I'm terribly sorry for the trouble. By the way, do you like it? It's finely made, don't you think?"

The landlady grinned strangely as she passed him a nameplate, a black background with *Sanshirō Tanimura* written in red letters.

Relieved, Tanimura accepted the nameplate bearing his name and quickly hung it on the board before hurrying down the guest house's stone steps.

***

The moon, high in the sky of Chang'an
The sound of clothes beaten on a wooden block
Ceaseless autumn winds
All things that remind me of Yumen Pass
I wonder when the northern barbarians will fall
And my husband will return from his long trip

Tanimura happily recited a Li Bai poem from a Tang-dynasty poetry collection he had avidly read over the summer.

There was a distance of over 500 meters between the house and the school, but it made an excellent walk to help Tanimura's digestion. On the way was a row of unimposing, sooty buildings: mahjong parlors, cheap cafes, fish markets, used bookstores, and billiards halls, among other things.

The weather that day was particularly good. In the sky an airplane buzzed by, a colorful advertisement trailing along behind it.

"Excuse me, do you mind if I ask you something?"

As Tanimura was walking beneath a row of trees on the street, reciting the poem to himself, he suddenly stopped and turned around in response to the young woman's voice, refreshing like the crickets you often hear in old-fashioned kitchens in the country.

"Would you...happen to know of a guest house named Seishūkan

27

with house number 61?"

*Seishūkan, I feel like I've heard that name before...*Tanimura thought self-consciously.

The woman had a longish bob cut and was carrying two large crimson-colored packages.

"Seishūkan"

"Yes!"

"By Seishūkan you mean..."

"Well, I've heard that a post office and Hachimangu shrine are nearby..."

Tanimura suddenly felt a warmth pulsing through his body.

"Wait...oh, I remember now. That's the...yes, I'm familiar with it."

"Oh really? I heard that it was a small guest house, and not being from around these parts I haven't the slightest idea where it is."

"Let me take you there."

"Well, that would be nice, but...are you on your way there now?"

"No, it's the other direction, but I have some time so we can go back together."

"I'm terribly sorry to trouble you..."

The leaves of the roadside sycamore trees rustled softly above Tanimura's head. He casually removed his hat in the cool breeze, but the flat-topped straw hat had yellowed from being worn all summer and made him feel a little embarrassed.

The woman with the bob cut looked like she might be a waitress. The powder on her neck had darkened, her face was bloated and pale. With well-defined eyes, eyebrows, and lips, she was extremely beautiful, and Tanimura had never walked side-by-side with such a young woman before, making it awkward to look directly at her.

"I will carry one of those packages for you. Please give me one."

"It is all right, I am fine."

A blue vein visible on the surface of the woman's beautiful finger looked uncomfortable, so Tanimura grabbed a package from the woman anyway. For some reason, this made him feel good.

"Oh, is that it?"

They climbed up the gentle slope of the Hachimangu road, and at the top of the hill was a white sign with the word "Seishūkan." Perhaps because he had just moved in last night, the wordless Tanimura had even forgotten the name of the guest house he was staying in.

"That's it."

Remembering the hair in his soup, Tanimura felt a pang of sadness.

"Thank you very much, I truly appreciate your help..."

It might have only been the sky reflecting in them, but the woman's eyes shone beautifully, seducing Tanimura's heart unlike anything he had felt before.

After reaching the guest house, he turned around and parted ways with the woman.

***

In the city, Tanimura's beloved evening lights were shining, casting a tint over everything. He was on his way back to the guest house, reciting a Li Bai poem even louder than before. A few lights glowed on the eaves of the house. At the bottom of the list of occupants posted on the building he saw his own name, Sanshirō Tanimura. He ran his eyes across the twelve or thirteen names, wondering which man the beautiful woman from earlier had come to visit, but not even a single one of the names seemed like the type of person she would have gone to see. The only one who seemed plausible was the kind-sounding name "Yuriko Komatsu."

"Yes! I suppose she must have come to visit a lady friend!"

Tanimura laughed pleasantly, relieved. But when he looked over at his nameplate, he noticed a single hair stuck to the letter "S" waving back and forth in the wind.

Tanimura turned melancholy again, remembering that undeniable, disgusting feeling when he had plucked a strand of the chubby girl's hair this morning. But then he realized he would surely be able to reprimand that chubby maid if he examined this newly discovered hair under the microscope, so Tanimura pulled off the hair stuck to his nameplate and went inside.

"Welcome back sir."

It was the chubby maid again.

Unlike this morning, her hair was now cleanly tied up, a thin layer of white powder on the back of her pig-plump neck, and lace surrounding the collar of her white cooking apron.

"Sir, shall I bring some food to your room shortly?"

Desiring to spend more time researching before dinner, Tanimura raised his voice in annoyance.

"I'm not hungry now. Come back in around an hour."

When the chubby maid glanced at Tanimura, she did not giggle like she had this morning, but instead sighed wistfully and went to go check on the mailbox. The squint-eyed maid, just returned from the second floor with a tray in hand, looked at him and grinned covertly as she headed to the kitchen.

Being extremely nearsighted, Tanimura failed to notice the second maid's grin and went off to the bathroom to wash his hands, sandals flip-flopping on the ground as he walked.

"Oh, hello!"

"Hi, about earlier..."

"No, it is I sir who should be thanking you. Because of your kindness, I was...by the way, did you come here to visit a friend?"

"No, actually I just moved here last night. And I had forgotten that 'Seishūkan was the name of the place I had moved into..."

She laughed politely. "Well then, easygoing sir, I'm in room number four on the second floor. Please stop by to see me."

"Yes, I would love to."

30

Tanimura, suddenly feeling giddy like a young boy, hurried back to his room with so much enthusiasm that he forgot to turn off the faucet. He rang the buzzer for the maid, thoughts of the microscope gone from his mind.

"Room service, how can I help you?"

"I'm getting hungry."

"Oh Tanimura, what a mean man you are! When I asked if I should bring food you said to wait an hour, and then as soon as I started to relax you rang the buzzer…"

"It's my fault. Just bring the food."

Tanimura laughed jovially again as he put grease in his hair.

***

It was the second dinner since Tanimura moved in. Although not a single dish was to his liking—fried baby tuna, daikon soup, fried tofu, miso-flavored vinegared scallions with konnyaku jelly—he nibbled on the scallions quietly while waiting impatiently for the chubby maid to bring the rice tub.

"Oh, I've been very busy."

"I thought I was fine, but I got terribly hungry."

"Hey! You're acting like a child."

The chubby maid placed a surprisingly small rice tub on the table, then thrust out a plump hand toward Tanimura.

"Well then, should I serve you some rice?"

"No thanks, I'll do it myself."

Ignoring his response, the maid served a bowl of rice to Tanimura with gentle movements. Later, the maid seemed to be lingering around, so Tanimura raised an eyebrow and spoke.

"That's all for now."

"Oh, all right…"

The chubby maid stuck a hand through her lace collar and into an inner pocket, withdrawing two small eggs that she placed upon Tanimura's tray.

"What are you doing?"

Face flushed, Tanimura stared at the eggs, but the maid had already left through the shoji doors.

For some reason, the sounds of women laughing and talking noisily came from the direction of the kitchen.

Even speaking from a medical point of view, Tanimura had no interest in chubby women like the maid, so he was puzzled as to how best to respond to her kind gift of eggs.

Returning them uneaten would probably incur the anger of the maid, so Tanimura placed the two tiny eggs into the wicker trunk which contained his clothes.

Unable to stop thinking about the beautiful woman on the second floor in room number four, Tanimura abruptly opened the door, went to the lobby, and purposefully made a loud racket as he went to the second floor.

Room number four was directly above his room. With a reserved attitude reminiscent of a cat, he lifted up his glasses.

"I'm sorry about earlier."

The lights appeared to be on inside the room, but it was utterly silent.

"I'm sorry about earlier," he repeated.

Right then, the paper door of the adjacent room slid open, and a bushy-eyebrowed man stuck out his head.

"It seems like the people in that room went out somewhere."

"Oh really..."

Tanimura felt his behavior to be completely foolish. He returned to his room, intending to study in earnest. On the way back down, he walked with tiny steps, like a rat, to conceal the sound of his footsteps. But it seems that no one had witnessed him going to the second floor, nor did anyone witness him coming back.

Upon returning to his room, he saw the food tray had been taken away. When he sat down calmly at his desk, the matter of the hair suddenly popped into his mind once again. So he quietly brought out the microscope and placed it under a light, used two fingers to pick out the strand of the chubby maid's hair sandwiched between the pages of his book, and began to examine it.

As before, there was still considerable mineral oil on the hair, but the texture was somehow different from the hair taken out of the mussel soup, much finer and much softer.

Wondering if the hair was actually from the squint-eyed girl, Tanimura suddenly felt a comically great affection for the chubby maid. She didn't possess a beautiful body or a beautiful face like the woman in room number four, but there was a certain attractive animalistic quality to her. But the moment he laid on the tatami mat to push a strange thought out of his mind, dust fell from the roof onto Tanimura's face—perhaps the occupants of room four above him had returned.

***

For the next few days, Tanimura was in a daze, not even attending school.

Whenever anyone moved about wildly on the second floor and dust fell, Tanimura would open his mouth wide like a madman and inhale deeply.

The beautiful woman didn't come to see him, even a single time. When he stumbled across her at the sink the next day, she was washing her hands. "I've been kind of busy lately, so I'm always out somewhere." Her tone even hinted that she might be purposefully avoiding Tanimura. However, despite not being able to see the woman anymore, a delightful memory of her lodged firmly in the corner of his mind.

33

Tanimura considered asking the chubby maid about the beautiful woman. But when he thought about the eggs, gradually pilling up in his wicker basket after every meal, he was struck with a terrible dread.

"You really don't have to bring me any more eggs. I simply don't like them very much."

Even if Tanimura were to say something like that to the chubby maid, she would probably think this man, polishing off two eggs each meal, was simply being kind.

"It's really no problem for me to bring two eggs for you each meal."

At a loss for what to do, Tanimura continued storing away two eggs into his basket each meal, as if part of his daily schedule.

It was a beautiful autumn night, the scent of the rain lingering in the air. In a sentimental mood, Tanimura stopped the chubby maid as she was passing by and asked about the woman in room number four.

"The woman in room four? Oh, you mean the painter woman who is a little overweight like me?"

"The overweight painter woman?"

"Yes."

"No, not her. There's a tall, slender woman there, isn't there? You know, with dark red lips and…"

"Oh, that person! That's somebody's wife."

Tanimura was in shock, as if a cold bucket of water was just splashed on his face.

Actually, if Tanimura were made to confess the truth, he had an inexpressibly sweet memory of his third time meeting that beautiful woman.

Having traveled far away from his hometown, and with his mother no longer living in this country, Tanimura had a habit of washing his underpants in the guest house's sink secretly, in the dead of night.

That night, when Tanimura went to the bathroom as usual to wash his two pairs of underwear, there was the sound of running water—someone was washing something in the sink. He continued nonchalantly into the bathroom. Of all people, the beautiful woman he had been obsessing over was in the middle of washing her face with cold water.

Tanimura put his underwear into his inner chest pocket at the exact same moment as the woman turned around, and the terrible state of confusion that ensued was as if a bundle of firecrackers had suddenly gone off at his feet.

"What happened to you?" Tanimura said.

"I was just weeping over a trifling matter…"

Perhaps it was because the bathroom had a long window with a view of the giant moon and dark roofs of the sleeping city—but there was something quaint and picturesque about the moment; even the way she spoke seemed terribly alluring.

"Why were you crying?" He said.

"No, I'm fine, really."

"But…you aren't fine, are you?"

Tanimura gazed intently into the woman's eyes, when suddenly she stood up under the dim electric light, like a delicate pink *nadeshiko* flower, and placed her cheek against his shoulder.

Tanimura felt a great agitation in his chest, like a roaring typhoon, and gently embraced the beautiful woman's well-rounded shoulders.

"Sir, would you mind loaning fifty yen to help a woman? I guarantee I will pay you back in the next few days. Alright?"

Tanimura hurriedly withdrew the money he had just received today and pushed it into the beautiful woman's tear-stained palm.

"Oh my! I will make sure to repay you no matter what. It was truly fate that brought us together!"

The beautiful woman tilted her head upwards and stood on tiptoes, eagerly awaiting Tanimura's lips. He tried with great effort to softly, gently press his lips onto hers, but she immediately pulled away and rested her head upon his furiously beating bosom for what felt like an eternity.

"Are you sure she's married?"

"Yes. Her husband has stayed in this guest house for a long time, you see, and had apparently sent her to one of those risqué *chabuya* places near Yokohama that caters to foreigners. But just recently he finally called her back."

"So is he still here?"

"No, he left money to reserve the room and moved with his wife to the outskirts of Tokyo, saying it was good for their health."

Tanimura could not help but become so annoyed that his head began to heat up. Unable to dare tell anyone about his depraved behavior, Tanimura seethed with anger.

He picked up the knife from his bookshelf and raged violently like a tiger, throwing the knife into the wall and cutting books to shreds. Being his first love, Tanimura's suffering seemed to be quite deep, and he lamented how meaningless it was to love a woman.

Just then, the chubby woman began to weep, her apron held up against her face.

"There's nothing for you to cry about."

"It makes me sad to see you going through all that."

"There's really no reason for you to pity me like that."

"Please forgive me."

"Hurry back to the kitchen now. There's no reason I should be asked to forgive you or anything like that…"

"But it's truly my fault!"

"You fool! Get away from me!"

The chubby maid gritted her teeth tightly and continued to cry.

More than the feeling he was about to lose his mind, it was the woman's intermittent wailing that grated on his nerves.

"Enough! You're being a real nuisance, I'm calling the landlady. I'm going to sulk alone to let my feelings run their course, and you're just getting in my way! I'm pressing the button now."

Grabbing his hand, the maid lowered her head to the floor as if prostrating herself before a god, then cried out.

"But I am in love with you! I'm so obsessed with you I could die…despite being laughed at by everyone, I'm in love with you!"

Tanimura was in utter shock. It was perhaps the great magnitude of this shock that caused his hysterical emotions to suddenly subside, only to be replaced with an unbearable desire to break out laughing.

"Please give me a chance," she said. "I may be an uneducated woman but I'll try my best, so let me spend my life with you."

Tanimura thought of the fifty-something eggs that had gathered in his wicker trunk, and a poem from his beloved Tang-dynasty poetry collection suddenly came to mind.

Our hearts are moved by not riches or fame, but the kindness of others. What need is there for selfish ambition?

Tears began to well up in his eyes.

Tanimura didn't consider himself particularly handsome, and he was going to graduate next year. After that he was planning on returning to his mountain village and becoming a doctor for farmers. *Who would fall in love with someone like me?* He suddenly felt a great emptiness well up from deep within him and remembered the numerous eggs given to him by the chubby maid. Then, overcome by emotion, Tanimura grabbed the maid's hand tightly.

"Oshige! Hey Oshige! I wonder where you have gone, all engrossed in your…"

The landlady's angry voice, its tone insinuating some wrongdoing, echoed all the way to Tanimura's room. A moment later—in what must have been someone's prank—the shrill sound of the buzzer rang out, *briiiiing.*

"Are you 'Oshige'?"

"Yes."

"I like that name."

The woman cried in short bursts, like a little girl. Her skin looked like that of a country woman, and even had a faint glow to it.

Hoping to offer some consolation to this poor woman, he began to talk about the hair he had found.

"You know what? The morning after I moved in, there was a strand of hair in my mussel soup. After thinking about it, I felt it must be yours, so that morning I casually plucked one of your hairs. I was planning on analyzing it with my microscope, you see…"

"Oh dear…."

"But it wasn't yours after all. You can relax, although the oil was the same type."

"Oh, I'm using the same inexpensive oil as Oshino…so that, that was the reason you plucked one of my hairs?"

With an exhausted expression like a wild animal, the chubby maid gazed intently at Tanimura's face.

***

After that, Tanimura's meals became much simpler fare. The two eggs that had been placed on his trays at breakfast or dinner disappeared completely, and the trays were now carried by the squint-eyed woman, with even more hairs to be found in his soups.

Tanimura reached the point where he would simply grin and remove the handful of hairs when he found them, having decided that it wasn't worth getting worked up over such a thing.

Our hearts are moved by not riches or fame, but the kindness of others. What need is there for selfish ambition?

Tanimura, inspired by the words of an ancient poem to believe that one's youth should not be wasted, tried to clear his mind by polishing his knives, wiping down his microscope, and flipping to a clean page in his notebook.

But then one day…

The route to school on a peaceful day made for an excellent walk, and Tanimura was in quite good spirits. As always, he was taking a stroll below the roadside trees, the autumn breeze in his hair.

"Well, well, is that not Tanimura?"

"Tanimura."

He lifted up his glasses and turned around. Standing before him was that beautiful woman who had been like a pretty pink *nadeshiko* flower, now slender like a rose.

Despite knowing he should remain claim, Tanimura's facial muscles began to twitch and his heart thumped within his chest.

"It's already been over three weeks," she said.

"So what business do you have with me?"

"I completely understand you being upset with me. Fortunately, my older sister won a prize in the autumn exhibition and benefitted by a great sum of money."

Before he realized it, they were walking side-by-side.

"When I dropped by here today, honestly worried you were upset with me, I was told that you had already moved out of town, and your new address wasn't known. This depressed me terribly, but just as I was walking around this area I happened to see you unexpectedly walking right past me…"

After all, that chubby maid was just a pig, thought Tanimura as he silently regretted grabbing hold of her hand that day. On the other hand, this beautiful woman told Tanimura how she borrowed money from him to buy art supplies for her sister, and walked around Ginza to gather funds for her sister's supplies.

Her arms were now outstretched, offering back the roughly seventy-yen he had loaned her, together with a handkerchief-wrapped package adorned with a pretty red ribbon.

Stunned, Tanimura accepted the items.

"Oh, I feel so much better now. This is the postcard with my sister's drawing on it. And by the way, you should come to Ueno this Saturday. She'd be delighted to have you come."

Tanimura eventually calmed down to the point where he could speak clearly again.

After drinking Orangeade with the woman at a fruit parlor they went their separate ways, and on the way home to his guest house Tanimura laughed harder than he had in ages. By the time he reached the guest house the lights had already begun to turn on, and he glanced over at the nameplate board posted under the front eave of the guest house. The nameplate labeled "Yuriko Komatsu" had been long removed, and each other room was occupied.

"Ah…the terror of a woman's single strand of hair…"

Tanimura gathered his trunk, his futon, and his other belongings, and though it was already dusk he summoned a cart and departed Seishūkan.

"Hey Driver, find me a nice and quiet guest house, please."

The only thing left to assuage Tanimura's feelings was the thought of how the chubby maid would dispose of the fifty-something eggs he had left behind in the closet at the guest house.

CONSOLATION

As a result of the drastic events of the last few months, even the beautiful city of Tokyo has gone through a series of shocking changes, the day-to-day activities of the dejected metropolis shattered into a million pieces, like myriad unfulfilled dreams. Stricken by the terrible memories of a long, hard war, wrinkles marred the faces of every person on the streets, even the younger folk, their vacant expressions a mixture of bitterness and disappointment.

It goes without saying that a majority of the houses were destroyed in the war, but above all obtaining food became extremely difficult. While it was true that anyone could buy a tiny sardine if they rounded up enough money, when you consider how that single sardine cost a full 40 sen, it becomes clear how exorbitant prices were. However, by this time the terrible war had already ended, and a proper order was gradually returning to things. There were very few houses in the bleak metropolis, and Jukichi was one those without a house. After his house in Asakusa burned down and he parted ways with his granddaughter Kiyoko, Jukichi was completely on his own. He tried visiting his younger brother's place in Shizuoka, but with such a large family they were struggling, so two weeks later Jukichi returned to Tokyo. Soon after, the war ended.

While he did not possess a house, Jukichi was relieved to learn of the war's end. In the face of a great defeat where unresolved conflicts remained, a host of miserable leaves were shaken off the tree of Japan, as if caught in a genuine divine wind, a *kamikaze*. Himself one of these fallen leaves, Jukichi had no choice but to continue living through these hard times in a state of shock.

Jukichi paused in front of the Yotsuya station and looked around. Unlike downtown, here buildings that had survived the fire dotted the landscape, hidden by clumps of trees. The structures of the Imperial Palace were dimly visible in the fog beyond a row of trees. Jukichi thought houses were such beautiful things. Whenever he gazed upon a clean, well-structured house, Jukichi couldn't help but feel that houses were humanity's ultimate form of luxury. Inside a house in the distance was a woman. He could vividly picture her, delighted that her house was one of the few that survived the fire, sending for her luggage to be returned from an evacuation site and happily unpacking her belongings.

Jukichi took out the cigarette butt he had picked up at Hibiya Park yesterday and inserted it into his bamboo pipe. Probably discarded by a foreigner, it gave off a pleasant-smelling smoke when lit. Over time Jukichi had grown quite skilled at finding cigarette butts, and when walking through a busy street could easily pick up five or six of them. Looking vacantly at houses in a residential area that had survived, he thought about Kiyoko. Jukichi had a strong desire to see her. The last time he had seen his granddaughter was the night of March 9th.

A short, but chubby girl, Kiyoko's tiny white teeth gave her an innocent, pretty smile. Being only seventeen, Jukichi thought there was no way she could survive. Not only were her whereabouts uncertain, but there were many casualties near Sumida Park where she and the others had taken refuge.

A train in terrible disrepair zipped by; a light jeep sped by. In the near twilight, a mist-like haze blanketed the charred city, transforming the crumbling gray concrete and red brick into a scene of beauty.

Jukichi's empty stomach caused dizziness from each puff of tobacco.

Walking was painful, but he couldn't stay in one place. Without a place to stay, if he didn't go to his friend's house in the next few days to pick up some food rations, Jukichi would go without food. His friend was still staying in a bunker in Tansumachi, Yotsuya. Living underground took a toll on his family, but without even the money to build a makeshift hut they had no choice but to continue lying down all day in a hole in the ground. Once a furniture maker, he had been enlisted as a factory worker by an airplane company in Ota, and as soon as the war ended he returned to his home to find it transformed into a bunker. Jukichi was himself a long-time furniture craftsman. Both men enjoyed catching fish and frequently went together on overnight fishing trips.

***

"Is Saburo there?"

"Oh, it's you, Jukichi…"

Saburo came out of the hole, red-faced. Sporting a well-built physique, he looked young enough to be Jukichi's son. Saburo was in fact much younger than Jukichi, but it was hard to believe Jukichi's age of 57. His body had deteriorated terribly, giving the appearance of a senior citizen in his 70s. With an unsightly bald head, missing front teeth, and a pointy jaw, Jukichi resembled an old dog. Befitting a furniture maker, his hands were the only youthful part of him left, with the rest of his body utterly haggard.

"There's not much to do, so I was having myself a drink."

"Oh…how brave of you. Black-market saké?"

"Yeah, something like that. I picked up around a liter for 80 yen, supposed to be a good deal."

The hole was only around five meters square, and packed with a jumble of items there was barely enough room to sit down. White powder came out of the boards serving as walls that were rotten so badly it seemed a single press of a finger would puncture a hole.

"This world has gone completely to shit. Four kilograms of potatoes are selling for fifteen yen, and I don't believe people are putting up with that."

"You couldn't be more right. But Saburo, you know things were different back in the day. Working at Kaneichi, picking up some mackerel pike at the market on the way home, not to mention getting a banana for only ten sen, then heading home and eating until your belly was full. It's just like seeing a ghost; a ghost you never believed in suddenly appears before you—that's how downright incomprehensible this crazy world has become. You still have a wife and kids, but Kiyoko is gone and I have nothing left. For me all that remains is simply living...but you know, I guess it's actually kind of interesting. After everything that's happened, I have no desire to end my life. I don't think I'm better off in the grave just because I'm lonely and alone. I'm terribly fortunate that I've never thought about anything like that. Spending our days doing nothing but eating steamed potatoes and sleeping like logs, it's hard to believe us humans are the supreme beings of creation, don't you agree?"

"Yeah, well...the fact is we're both alive, and that in itself is incomprehensible...All right then, have a drink. I won't feel right if you don't at least drink to cheer yourself up and keep on living. After all, we managed to escape injury and are now spending our days like this inside a hole in the ground."

"Well said. Ahh, this is some good saké. I'm curious how much one drink goes for. Each sip is like pouring water onto hot ashes and watching a great cloud of steam rise up. It stings and numbs my tongue, Saburo. Definitely some good saké. You know, saké is the best medicine. I'm really curious how much one drink goes for. Thanks so much."

Jukichi took out his collection of cigarette butts and put them on the table. Saburo immediately grabbed them and set them alight.

"Where is your family?"

"They went out to Funabashi City to buy some fish."

"You're very fortunate to have money."

"We don't have any money. It's mostly gone, and we'll be lucky if we last another month."

While burning twigs in the small cooking stove, Saburo occasionally offered Jukichi another drink. Thanks to an empty stomach, Jukichi got inebriated quickly.

"Things were interesting, back in the good old days…"

"They sure were."

"We'll never return to those days…"

"Yeah, they're not coming back. Those damn companies got together and messed everything up. I was fooled countless times by those newspapers. They talked constantly about how we were winning, because of course talking about winning increased readership. Those stupid newspapers would write about our great military achievements every single day, like a broken record. And I totally fell for it."

"Ahh, nothing beats good saké. I haven't had any saké like this in quite a while because I've been living on my own. I even thought I wouldn't be able to come here any longer to pick up food rations. I've also been running out of money and don't have anything to wear either. But if only Kiyoko would have been around, things would have turned out differently."

"Kiyoko sure was good-looking. A real good girl. Long ago, in Akasaka there was this Geisha named Manryu, and Kiyoko looked just like her photograph. She had a rounded, pretty face. But if she hasn't come back yet, she must be dead."

"Yeah, but I just can't see her being dead. That's why I haven't sent in her death certificate yet. I can't help feeling she's still alive. Just the other day when I was at Nihonbashi in the evening, you see, there was this girl riding in a jeep. I only caught a glimpse of her in passing, but she was a spitting image of Kiyoko. However, this girl was wearing brown clothes. On that night in March, Kiyoko was wearing violet work pants so I guess it was a different person. But sometimes I think

Kiyoko, unable to even find something to eat, is off dancing somewhere...After all, she was born in Asakusa and tends to like crowded places like that...Oh, by the way, we haven't gone fishing together in a long time. I'd like to go out fishing somewhere with you, Saburo..."

"Yeah, that's true. I'd like to figure out a way to go fishing, too. Unlike you, I was able to take my fishing equipment with me so it escaped the fire."

Jukichi was pleasantly drunk. Snacking on roasted soybeans as he drank, each time he closed his eyes blurry rainbow-colored images appeared, like visions of a fantastic undersea palace, and then vanished into nothingness. And yet, as he ruminated over the events of his long life, as a cow would chew its cud, Jukichi could no longer tolerate the bitterness and began to sing quietly to himself.

"You sure seem to be in a good mood."

"Oh, I'm feeling great. Everyone needs friends...But actually, getting drunk has depressed me."

Jukichi wiped his tears with a clenched fist. He felt an intense yearning to see Kiyoko. Overwhelmed by the misery of living homeless, going from place to place, he let his head fall forward and rested his forehead on the table.

***

After receiving three sardines from his friend's wife, who had just returned from Funabashi, Jukichi wrapped up various items in cloth, including potatoes and food rations, strapped them to his back and headed back to the city, which was already in near darkness. The most beautiful lights that civilization had left behind flickered here and there in the devastated city. From somewhere came the sound of a steam train. The *toot* of the train's whistle rang out mournfully over a scorched field and out towards the night sky. It was silent all around, except for the occasional passing car or train, as if declaring that Tokyo's nights would remain desolate for all eternity. Jukichi stumbled through thick fog on his way to Yotsuya Mitsuke.

"Hey mister, you dropped something."

Startled, Jukichi glanced behind him. A young man, probably a college student, stood there lighting a cigarette. Jukichi suddenly had an urge to smoke. He regretted leaving his cigarettes behind in Tansumachi.

"Thank you very much…"

Jukichi halted for a moment, watching the young man set fire to his cigarette. He couldn't help but envy the college student smoking a fresh, tightly wrapped cigarette. Tobacco rations were the one thing he failed to get a hold of, so for some time now Jukichi had a hankering for a fresh cigarette.

"It sure is a nice evening."

Startled, the student gazed past Jukichi as if he could see through him. "You look like you're feeling quite good."

"I was drinking," Jukichi said with a chuckle.

"Is there somewhere to get a drink around here?"

"Well, let's see…I was called over to my friend's place, and…"

"Oh really? How lucky of you."

Presumably having no interest in a staggering drunk man, the student took a glowing red puff or two of his tobacco, stuffed his hands in his overcoat pockets and hurried away towards Ichigaya.

Jukichi dropped another potato. Somehow he lacked the energy to pick it up. Jukichi no longer cared; he was utterly sick and tired of everything. All he wanted to do was have a cigarette—to deeply inhale a thick, swirling cloud of smoke like it was the very air he breathed.

A trolley sped noisily past him.

"That's right, I said I would part with those boots for a thousand yen."

"A thousand yen for something you got free from a soldier?"

"I want to sell at a high price because I got them for free."

Two young women chatted as they strolled down the street, each carrying a large bundle. Jukichi was tired of walking. The quiet night air had gotten chilly, and the effects of the alcohol were starting to wear off. He found a place that looked like it would offer shelter from the cold—the ruins of a stone wall damaged by fire—and set down his things. His mood improved now that the load was taken off his shoulders. Oh, how great it felt to be able to move freely again. When carrying such a heavy load, everything tended to upset him. Hugging his knees, Jukichi began to doze off. A vision came to him of Kiyoko in old-fashioned attire: a red pleated skirt with a ribbon in her hair.

The elegant notes of a piano drifted in from a radio somewhere. Even in the desolate night, a whisper of the old metropolis floated in the mist. The defeated beauty of a defeated country flashed by for an instant, like a gust of wind. With defeat came the loss of everything that made the city what it was. Like the transformation of a long, powerful snake to a tiny, unsightly caterpillar, the utterly miserable condition of this city had more power to persuade the nation's people than the most eloquent speeches of a hundred politicians. Despite the stirrings of movement or the flow of people, despite the bitter defeat, the city continued on deeper into the night.

A little while later, Jukichi had another visitor.

"Hey, mister, not feeling too well?"

Before him stood a young boy of around twelve or thirteen wearing a baggy national uniform.

"I'm feeling perfectly fine."

"You drunk?"

"I ain't drunk."

"Stupid old man."

"I *am* a stupid old man."

"You're a crow!"

"Oh…caw caw!"

The boy put his foot on Jukichi's shoulder, like he was going to get

48

his shoe polished…but Jukichi opened his eyes impassively and quietly brushed aside the boy's foot.

"You're suffering from malnutrition, old man…"

"You shouldn't be wandering around like this. Your family is waiting at home for you."

"I don't have a home. It burned down."

"Oh, so your house burned down too."

"It sure did. It burned down good and clean, leaving nothing but ashes…"

"Where was it?"

"Ginza."

"Oh, Ginza…"

The boy grabbed Jukichi's bundle and hurried off into the darkness. Jukichi simply stared in silence, watching him go. He thought the boy might have had a cigarette, and regretted not asking him for one.

A light breeze began to blow. In the fog, a single red light was visible. Jukichi stood up. He didn't feel like walking but the light was a good distance away.

Jukichi withdrew his wallet from his waist pocket and took out a ten sen bill under the light. He was fully aware that he had to return to Asakusa. Hunger caused an uncomfortable sensation in his chest. Jukichi took the remaining roasted soybeans from his pocket and tossed them into his mouth. As he chewed, the tiny beans bursting with each bite, Jukichi was happy for at least having survived. In Asakusa, a disturbing number of people had lost their lives. Innumerable people had been burned to death in a disaster even worse than an earthquake, and thinking about how he was still alive made Jukichi beam with joy. It was a relief just to have the incessant rain of fire from those massive airplanes stopped. Jukichi himself didn't have a single enemy, so there was no reason he ever would go to battle against those large airplanes. He didn't know anything about the rest of the world, so he thought there was no reason to make so many children into soldiers and send them off to war. Jukichi longed for the Tokyo of the past. He

49

remembered how there was a butcher named Mikawaya near Yotsuya Mitsuke. Long ago there was an eel restaurant named Sanukiya. On the road that he was hobbling down, the air raids hadn't left even a trace of the past.

Jukichi missed his pretty granddaughter whom Saburo had said resembled the geisha Manryu, and was tormented by a loneliness so terrible that he wanted to throw up his arms in despair.

Jukichi's bald head struck the ground hard like a chunk of metal. He squinted, an odd expression on his face as if about to burst out laughing. There was a blindingly bright light. A heavy object passed across his outstretched legs, making a great creaking sound. Jukichi groaned as his entire body burned hot like a flame. A sharp, incomprehensible pain surged through him, but it immediately abated, giving way to an intense pleasure that filled his body. The ground smelled of oil. He thrashed around as if begging for mercy. As he slowly lost consciousness, blood began oozing out of his body. Even the railroad tracks began to glisten, attesting to the great amount of blood.

It was a terrible way to get injured, like a soldier who had fought in a trench to the very last moment. But Jukichi felt Kiyoko's hand, and heard her sweet voice.

"Grandfather, you're being silly sleeping at a place like this. Let's hurry home and have something warm to eat..."

"Our house was burned to the ground a long time ago. Foolish girl, where have you been? You worried me terribly..."

He heard a clamor coming from somewhere above. It sounded like distant voices, but at the same time might have been the chirping of cicadas on a bright summer day.

Time gradually passed and the night gradually brightened, but the city remained still. The moonlight, which had begun to shine out across the land in the evening, had intensified as the night wore on, and now all was bright as if the ground was blanketed in snow. On a trench's gently sloping bank Jukichi lay under a straw mat, ragged rubber socks on his protruding feet. It seemed like a tragic way to die,

Jukichi laying on his back with a straw mat covering his face, as if he had died an honorable death. And yet it was not such a terrible way to die; on the contrary, his life could not have ended in a more fortunate manner, laying there like a rock for a very long time in the midst of a vast expanse of nature.

Before long, when dawn broke the city would undoubtedly begin to repeat the events of the previous day, and the steam train would blow its whistle as always.

As for Saburo, in all likelihood he would eventually go fishing by himself.

THE CRANE'S FLUTE

Once, a long, long time ago, there was a year of great famine. There was a village, and in the village lived many cranes. The cranes wandered around day after day searching for food, but since there was no food to be found anywhere, the impatient cranes gathered their belongings and traveled far away.

And so, all that remained in the village was a crane with an injured leg and his wife. The injured crane stood on the edge of a once crowded, yet now deserted swamp where the reeds grew thickly, and he gazed up into the sky where the other cranes had flown off to.

Then one day, the crane wife was prodding desperately with her beak along the water's edge, searching for something to eat. Tottering on weak legs, she searched hopelessly about here and there, hoping to find at least a tiny fish, even a measly loach. The morning light sparkled brightly, with a single cloud floating lazily through the expansive sky, heading westward. Within a forest of young trees, the sunlight filtered down through the leaves and fell gently on the ground in patches, forming a picturesque scene.

Sometime later, the inexpressibly beautiful tone of a flute rang out through the forest. "Oh my, what could that be?" thought the crane. As she stood there listening to the lovely sound of the flute, her stomach that had been empty suddenly felt full.

The crane quietly moved in the direction of the flute's sound until she discovered, lo and behold, that it was being played by the crane with the injured leg.

"Oh, it was *you* that was playing the flute?" asked the crane wife.

With a look of embarrassment the injured crane turned to face his wife. "A few minutes ago, I thought there might be something around here and began to search the swamp. Then my beak struck something hard with a *clink*, and when I hurriedly picked it up the object turned out to be this flute. Wondering what it was, I tried putting it in my mouth different ways until all of a sudden a beautiful sound came from its tiny hole, and as I played the flute I forgot all about my hunger…"

"Oh, is that what happened? I was surprised by the flute's pretty sound. Pleasant memories from long ago somehow popped into my head, and a wonderful feeling came over me."

The flute's tone was so beautiful that the two cranes felt silly for having always worried about not having food.

Bearing a grudge against the many cranes that had flown away without any regard for them, the two cranes had spent their days complaining. But once they obtained the flute, with its exceptionally beautiful tone, they became satisfied with what little food they had, and from then on only spoke about pleasant memories and how they wished good fortune for the cranes who had gone far away.

"You know, when I'm listening to that flute," said the wife, "I am no longer discouraged, even a little, and I grow hopeful that soon we will enter a time very different from this miserable famine, where the crops are bountiful every year. Today I am heading to a place a short distance away to search for fish, so now and then please play the flute for me."

"Of course. But be careful to not get injured on the way."

The crane wife immediately took flight. A little while later, she came to a small pond. Something was splashing around in the pond. Wondering what it might be, she set her sights on the pond and flew down to the ground to discover a place where many fish gathered of

53

the likes never before seen. Heart beating fast, she grabbed one of the fish. Carrying the souvenir for her husband, the crane wife immediately headed towards the sound of the flute, when she encountered a family of cranes with three children coming in from the west.

"Oh dear, it's been quite a while. What happened to you all?" asked the crane wife.

"Well, we have had such a terrible time. Wherever we went there was hardship, and two of our children even passed away from illness. Just as we were wandering around, hoping to find a suitable place, we heard the inexplicably beautiful sound of a flute, and so we came here, thinking that there must be something good wherever the flute was being played," said one of the parents.

"My, were you truly able to hear the flute's sound from such a great distance? That flute is being played by my husband, who has an injured leg."

Guided by the crane wife, the family of cranes flew for a while, and were surprised to see the very village that they had abandoned. Having listened to the flute's sound for a long time, the crane wife felt carefree and accepting of all things, finding pleasure in helping others no matter how bad off she and her husband were.

Without delay the crane wife took the fish she had caught and served it up for dinner, feeding it to the crane family, tired and hungry from their journey.

After taking only a single bite of the food, both the injured crane and his wife said insistently, "Please help yourself to the food. Eat plenty and regain your strength before you go," and upon hearing this, the parents began to tear up. Until recently all the cranes—thinking only of themselves and hiding food from others—would fight over food whenever they came into contact, cruelly deceiving and hurting each other, and as a result the cranes, constantly concerned about food, never had even a single cheerful day.

The cranes would form groups, clamoring loudly, and prey on the weak; the strong would brag of the paltry food that they seized.

Naturally, even the behavior of the young cranes degenerated as they mimicked only the worst traits of the adults, using foul language and constantly getting in fights. The famine had stretched on for so long that everyone had abandoned their village, but now the village was even more peaceful than before, with the seven cranes talking amongst themselves about living and working together happily, never giving up hope no matter what happened.

Thanks to the crane wife they discovered a place with many fish, so the seven cranes were always able to have enjoyable meals as they lived simple lives.

Then one night, when a spectacular moon was high in the sky, a golden light radiated brightly all around, so the injured crane began to play the flute once more.

The three crane children turned towards the moon and felt a strong urge to sing.

"Wow, what a pretty, pretty moon that is…"

The youngest child began to sing. Then the second youngest boy began to sing as well, "The village where you were born is the best." The oldest boy joined in. "What a pleasant night. I can't help but enjoy myself."

"Indeed, we are happy now," said the mother crane leisurely. "Just considering that you three are no longer starving, I'm glad we came back here. But if only some of the other cranes were to come home too, things would be much livelier."

Puffing on his pipe, the father crane listened carefully to the flute played by the injured crane. It sang out with a bright, clear tone—*tweetely tweet*.

"Oh my, I hear the noisy sound of someone's wings flapping. Perhaps another crane has returned home."

Before long, the cranes who had abandoned the village returned, one after another, lured by the flute's sound.

"We gladly welcome back anyone who is not arrogant and shares their food with others," said the crane with the injured leg.

Overjoyed, the cranes who had returned broke out in tears.

Then they all went to work, and everyone shared their food amicably among the group...Perhaps even to this day, the land of cheerful, lovely cranes is still around somewhere.

Our hearts are always pure
Poor we may be, but inside we are abundant
Sharing together
Working together
Always with pure hearts
We go on, loving each other

So went the gentle melody of the crane's flute—*tweetely tweet*.

EMPLOYMENT

She didn't understand why she was so angry. Sitting upon the roots of a pine tree, Sakiko gathered pebbles from the ground and screamed out as she tossed them towards the ocean, throwing like a boy. The pebbles only went a short way before falling onto the nearby sand with a dull thud.

On the winter seashore, strong gusts of wind blew in occasionally from the distance. Despite there being no clouds in sight, soft beams of light fell from the sky onto the beach, like scattered needles. Sakiko fell down abruptly onto the sandy ground, rolling around and kicking up bits of dry sand like a dog thrashing about. The sand came in contact with her hot body at her neckline, her sleeves, and the hem of her skirt. The sensation of sand accumulating on her sweaty body felt good. Eventually she thrust out her chest and poured dry sand all over it. The sand smelled of salty seawater. She even tried scooping up a pile of sand with both hands, saying "It's shower time!" as she sprinkled it onto her knees. Now and then small, barely visible tornados, like breezes from a miniature world, blew sand gently onto her cheeks. The sand on her knees was also blown and scattered by the wind, leaving two round knees glowing faintly red in the sun.

All of a sudden, Sakiko jumped to her feet upon the beach. Both her back and chest were encrusted with sand. Sakiko shook her hair to try to dislodge the sand and then ran home, holding her breath to prevent even a single grain of sand from coming off her body.

In the second-floor sunroom, Ken'ichi watched the sand-covered Sakiko come running in from the beach and hurried down the stairs to see what was going on.

"Saki, what happened to you? Your cheeks are all puffed up..."

The moment Ken'ichi entered the porch Sakiko muttered, "Hurry, hurry...", making a face as if she was about to throw up. She rushed into the living room and Ken'ichi hurried after her, unsure how to react. Once inside, she turned around and stared at him for a few moments, then suddenly removed her coat and tabi socks, and violently patted down her entire body. The sand lodged inside her neckline, sleeves, and hem sprinkled onto the fresh tatami mat.

"What happened to you?"

"You know what...I brought you a souvenir..."

Sakiko's face was pale as she shook her body. Ken'ichi simply stared at her in astonishment. Sakiko untied her belt, tossed it on the floor, and hurried off to her room. Ken'ichi gazed at the sandy tatami mat for a few seconds, when all of a sudden he felt something burning in his chest. Ever since yesterday it seemed like Sakiko, feeling lonely, had been blaming him for something. Ken'ichi had gone earlier to search for Sakiko on the beach, but he returned empty-handed, unable to find her. He stood dumbfounded in the living room for a few moments, but deep down his love for Sakiko gripped him tightly.

Ken'ichi headed over to Sakiko's room. She had already changed and was wiping her face with a wet washcloth.

"Hey, I'm sorry about earlier..."

Ken'ichi was silent.

"Are you upset?"

"Why should I be upset? There's nothing to be upset about. By the way, I tried going to the beach a little while ago, but..."

"Really? I was on a long walk, very far away..."

Sakiko looked at Ken'ichi reflected in the mirror and giggled.

Without warning Ken'ichi squatted down, put his arm around Sakiko's shoulder, and kissed her forehead. Wet washcloth in hand, she rested her head against his chest, but a moment later jumped up, screaming.

"Stop! Stop it! Stay away from me! I hate you, Ken'ichi, I really hate you!" she said, tossing the washcloth at Ken'ichi's reflection in the mirror. Then she got up and, leaning against the wall, began spouting out words at an amazing speed.

"Just go off to Changchun city or wherever you want! How could you make plans to go to a place like that without asking me? And why do you have to go to such a remote place like Changchun? Did you go to college just to get a job there?"

Ken'ichi said nothing. The petite, small-faced Sakiko looked to Ken'ichi like a schoolgirl. He couldn't believe she was actually 21 years old.

"You dummy, why don't you come see me in Changchun? It's not like we'll never see each other again."

"Why would you ever get a job at a place that's so far away? It's all because my sister went away, right? I don't believe you care at all about what I think. And that really irritates me…"

Just then, the shrill alarm of the desk clock rang out. Sakiko grabbed the clock in annoyance. Shocked by her hysterical behavior, Ken'ichi stared dumbfoundedly at Sakiko. She opened the window and tossed out the clock, still ringing loudly, into the yard. A chilly breeze blew in from the window, and the roar of the sea sounded like thunder rolling in the distance.

Ken'ichi went through the hallway and into the yard to pick up the clock that had been tossed outside. He did understand Sakiko's feelings—in fact, until a week ago he himself couldn't have imagined ever getting a job in a place like Changchun. He had been planning on working in Tokyo after graduation and had even asked the college's employment advisor to send out his resumes to Mitsui, Mitsubishi, and Tokyo Dentō. But Ken'ichi ended up suddenly giving up on those opportunities and instead got employed with a certain steel manufacturing company in Changchun, Manchuria.

It wasn't simply the capriciousness of youth—there was some great surge of emotion compelling his young heart. Rather than stay here in the tiny country that was Japan, clinging to a small chair, he yearned to travel to a distant land and work to his heart's content. Changchun was a fresh, emerging city, and the idea of working in the steel manufacturing industry, now in a time of rapid development during the war, had a certain appeal to Ken'ichi.

As expected, Sakiko's parents were shocked when he broached the topic of employment in Changchun, and had trouble understanding why Ken'ichi would want to go to such a distant place.

Once Ken'ichi brought the clock back to Sakiko's room, in a drastic change of attitude she quietly picked the clock up and began to wind it up very, very slowly.

"My decision to go to Changchun has nothing to do with Katsuko. Of course I really liked that girl, and I would have made her my wife if I could, but she already got married to someone else and moved away…But I don't think I can afford to keep thinking about Katsuko forever. I searched for a job far away because, to be honest, I've grown to dislike Tokyo…Saki, I don't expect you to understand my reasons for leaving Tokyo, ther place where I was born, but nevertheless I want to get away from here and see what it's like out there. I simply decided that I want to try working in a new place with real potential…I just can't stand Tokyo anymore!"

"So…that means you don't like me either, right?"

"Well, of course I…Saki, you're not making this easy for me. I like you, I really like you, but my aversion to Tokyo has nothing to do with you, and…I don't know how to explain this…but when a man decides on his career, you see, I think there's something altogether different than relationships with girls, consideration for others' feelings, and so on…I no longer think of Changchun as being such a distant place, and I wish you would come visit me there sometime. But the thing is, I just want to work in a place where I feel at ease. That's why I wish you would just be happy for me..."

Sakiko was silent.

Having such a wonderful man go off to such a remote place...I won't stand for it, I just won't stand for it! Keeping silent, Sakiko stared up angrily at Ken'ichi. He had those sturdy shoulders, and hidden behind those plastic, thin-framed glasses were those friendly eyes, always staring out into space, not to mention that squared-off jaw, which Sakiko found attractive and symbolized Ken'ichi's strong will. Even assuming they were going to part ways, Sakiko was reluctant to end things with only a kiss on the forehead—and just thinking about how today would be the last time they saw each other made her angry and want to roll around in the sand like earlier. Her mother and the others were planning to come on an evening train. But now it seemed like Sakiko and Ken'ichi arriving to this summer house in Chiba ahead of everyone else was meaningless. Behind the bathroom, the tenant farmer who managed the summer house was singeing hairs of chicken skin over a bonfire.

"So, I guess tomorrow is our last day."

"Yeah..."

"You know, I'm really sorry."

"There's nothing to apologize for. Saki, you've done many things for me...and for that, I am very grateful."

Around six in the evening, Sakiko's family arrived. Nakahori and Sakurauchi came on the same train. With both of her younger brothers here, the once peaceful summer house became a place of bursting excitement. Suffering from poor health, Sakiko had been here since autumn to recuperate, but she had just returned this week from an infrequent visit to Tokyo. Having not wanted to part so quickly with Ken'ichi in Tokyo, she rode the steam train with him this morning from Ryogoku. Despite Ken'ichi's busy schedule, Sakiko invited him to a farewell party at their house in Chiba.

"Oh my, did someone let in a dog? The floor is covered with sand..."

Taking a look at the sand strewn about on the tatami mat, Sakiko's mother headed to the kitchen to grab the broom. "Sakiko, how did all this sand get here?"

Sakiko exchanged a glance with Ken'ichi and smiled. In spite of the cold weather, both Nakahori and Sakurauchi leaned against the fence in the yard while gazing out at the sea, saying they hadn't seen the ocean in ages. Both her brothers wore school uniforms, and only Ken'ichi was dressed up in a suit.

"All right boys, it's chilly out there so please come inside. We turned the charcoal brazier on..."

With the floor swept clean and cushions gathered from the neighborhood laid out nicely, Sakiko's mother put a large pot on the brazier.

"Hey, you two. I said to come inside. You'll catch a cold..."

Carrying Takashi, Sakiko's other little brother, Ken'ichi called from the porch to the two boys at the fence. Sakiko wore a dark-colored ribbon in her hair, and a fancy silk crepe coat over her clothes. With cheerless facial features like those of a Kyoto doll, her pale skin had an oddly miserable appearance.

When Nakahori and Sakurauchi came inside, Sakiko purposefully sat between the two college students. Ken'ichi glanced over and was actually relieved to see Sakiko, smiling brightly as she took a seat not beside himself, but on the other side of the room.

"So Sakurauchi, where did you decide on?"

"Decide on? You mean my place of employment?"

"Yes."

Sakurauchi stuttered in a peculiar manner as she spoke; born in Kagoshima, she apparently had trouble getting rid of her regional accent.

"I ended up getting a position at an iron manufacturing plant in Yawata, but it's a little depressing since I don't know anyone there..."

"Wow, you are going to Yawata? What about Nakahori?"

"I'm going to Jilin for The South Manchuria Railway," said Nakahori. "It's quite a distance away, but since Ken'ichi is going to Changchun I'm looking forward to seeing him once in a while..."

"Oh, you're really traveling a great distance...I thought Changchun, where Ken'ichi was going, was far away, but Nakahori's job is even farther..."

The vegetables and pieces of chicken inside the pot began to boil. While feeding Takashi bit by bit from the pot, Ken'ichi bounced the child upon his knee. Sakurauchi had a close-cropped haircut and a masculine figure, but her eyelids were puffy, and when she smiled a double tooth gave her a childish appearance. Nakahori had a quiet demeanor, as if better suited to be a public servant, hair slicked down and a clean collar on his college uniform. His skin was dark, and a large nose typified his good-natured personality.

"It looks like next year everyone is moving far away..." Sakiko said as she poured beer for everyone, hands moving awkwardly.

Unlike the others, Sakurauchi said she preferred saké to beer, so they had asked the summer house's landlord to purchase some locally brewed saké for her in advance. After eight o'clock, Ken'ichi's friend Nobeoka who worked at the Kisarazu train station stopped by. A middle school ex-classmate, Nobeoka was an outspoken man with a raspy voice. He had the personality of a typical station attendant, but was well-liked for his candid, amusing way of speaking. Nobeoka wore a plain hakama skirt below his coat.

"Ken'ichi, you're going to Changchun, right? I'm utterly jealous of you...I wish I could go off somewhere far away like that. If I only had graduated college like you, I'd have some employment choices at nice locations. But having only graduated middle school, I'm out of luck."

Nobeoka gradually became inebriated and before long was clenching his gaunt fist above his knees, loudly declaring, "Sure, I fix train tracks and am basically a construction worker, but soon I'm going to find a great job! I'll show you!" Sakurauchi grew increasingly annoyed with Nobeoka—a young man displaying the audacity of a country-dweller by bragging how he would make it big at any moment—and suddenly fell silent as she gulped down her saké.

"Well, after graduating college things get really tough...up until now you all have been able to go in circles, like riding a merry-go-round within the limits of the ideologies you learned in school, but us young folk have to figure out our own ideologies, right? It's important that we discover our ideologies on our own..."

"Interesting. So I guess you mean that *you* are the only one who has your own ideologies? What kind of ideologies are they anyway?"

Sakurauchi turned pale, squinted her puffy eyes, and glared hard at Nobeoka. Something like seething anger was visible in her face.

Sakiko's mother laid out futons for the college students on the second floor, then took back the sleepy Takashi and quickly withdrew into Sakiko's room. By this point, Ken'ichi seemed to be regretting inviting Nobeoka, but he also hesitated to butt into their conversation, so he kept quiet for the time being.

"Are you really that obsessed with academic learning? I don't know what you mean by 'go in circles within the limits of the ideologies learned in school', but tonight is the farewell party for Ken'ichi and I, so enough with the highbrow conversation!"

"Ha ha ha...You call *this* highbrow conversation?"

Nobeoka laughed pleasantly as he thrust chopsticks into the boiling pot. The next moment Sakurauchi screamed out, "You jerk! Who do you think you are insulting!" grabbing Nobeoka's chopsticks and throwing them at the glass door. Nobeoka jumped up, enraged. The instant he got up he grabbed a nearby beer bottle and threw it at Sakurauchi's head with all of his might. Right as Sakurauchi laid down on the tatami mat to evade the projectile, the beer bottle smashed hard into the wall of the alcove. Sakurauchi raised her face, blood flowing from her nose down to her chin and lips; the beer bottle had apparently struck her nose. Everything happened so quickly that Ken'ichi, Nakahori, and Sakiko were all in a breathless stupor.

After Sakurauchi wiped the blood with her right hand, she quickly grabbed Nobeoka by the collar, raised up the glass door of the porch, and jumped down onto the sand with him. There were sounds of a violent struggle and a cheek being slapped several times. Through it all, the roar of the sea continued.

"Hey! That's enough, stop it already…"

Nakahori went out on the porch, but the two were grappling with each other tightly, rolling around on the sand. Ken'ichi also came out on the porch but stood frozen, quietly watching the quarrel. Hidden deep in the delight of finding a job was the loneliness of leaving the life of a student and going to a far-off place, away from friends and family; it was this that caused their irritation over the last month—a feeling that was a mix of frustration and the desire to be pampered. The scene of Sakurauchi fighting with all of her strength seemed to Ken'ichi like a wonderful display of pent-up emotions, and watching it was truly refreshing. When it came down to a fight, Kagoshima-born Sakurauchi was trained in karate, so Nobeoka didn't have a chance. After a few pushes and shoves, Nobeoka ended up pinned below Sakurauchi, the young man groaning as his throat was being choked.

"Hey Sakurauchi, that's enough already, cut it out!"

Nakahori slipped on his clogs and went down into the yard. Face covered with snot and saliva, Nobeoka ground his teeth and moaned.

"I'll never lose to a stupid college student!" Nobeoka cursed, even as he was being choked. When he heard that, Ken'ichi, wearing only socks, jumped down into the yard and separated the two.

"Nobeoka! Go home, you asshole!" Ken'ichi roared. Nobeoka stood up, revealing a bare chest and a drop of blood on the corner of one eye. He took a few breaths that reeked of saké as he stared down Sakurauchi, but soon hurried out of the yard, barefoot.

"Look, there's a hat over there…"

Sakiko brought in the hat she found, but nobody would go return it to Nobeoka.

"What a rude guy. Why did you invite a jerk like that?" Sakurauchi complained to Ken'ichi. Sakiko's mother was still in a state of mild shock from everything, but she soon brought over a cloth and handed it to Ken'ichi. He in turn passed it to Sakurauchi, and then took off his socks before going inside. A little while later he heard what sounded like Nobeoka singing as he walked across the distant coastline, voice faint as if drowned out by the wind.

"He's a good guy at heart, but living in the country makes people overly self-conscious and distorts their personality like that..."

"I don't know what happened but he sure is a peculiar guy, unbearably old-fashioned, and that know-it-all attitude is unfitting for a man. How old is he, anyway?"

"I guess he's around 25, but Nobeoka has a serious inferiority complex, which I hadn't realized until now...He used to frequently brag that he got a proper job before me, but I didn't know he was that simple-minded...But I wonder, when each of us travels far away and works at a company for a while, will we also become be corrupted like that?"

"Not to mention he's an angry drunk..."

"Yeah, although he's actually pretty interesting when he's not drinking. He's a truly mellow, amiable guy..."

"I guess it's best he's only working at a station. Who wants to be around a guy that takes offense at everything and picks fights, you know?"

The next morning, Sakiko was sunbathing in the small sunroom on the second floor. She lay half-naked on a rattan reclining chair, her back towards the sun, quietly reading a book. Yesterday's turbulent waves of youth had become calm and peaceful, like the gentle waves outside of the window.

A group of three young men and three young women sailed upon a white pleasure boat departing from the city of Rüdesheim, heading downstream along the Rhine river. This group of student actors had done a series of performances upstream the Rhine with only the six of them, but attendance was poor, so by the time they arrived at Rüdesheim they were so short on money they could only afford lodging expenses, lacking the funds to even buy bread. At that time, an elderly gentleman riding a horse in the hotel's garden took pity on these dejected young people and invited them to the island of Nonnewelt, which offered a spectacular view of seven mountains and the bustling city of Königswinter downstream. Of the three young women, Genma won the heart of the wealthy elderly gentleman. She worried over what to do about him until they arrived at a city downstream, but in the end she forsook his love, coming ashore the harbor town with Guiel, one of the three young men, where she faced a life of need and uncertainty, and the precious days of youth…

After finishing Schmidtbonn's "Beyond the Mountains", Sakiko rested her face on the book, engrossed in a whirlpool of emotions. Below her cheeks were the white pages of the book, but she imagined the deep, cold water of the Rhine flowing lazily below the words on those pages. Sakiko also fantasized about becoming a young lady just like the character Genma. The young men and women appearing in the book had a resilient courage to confront an ongoing life of need and uncertainty. But then why did life seem so gloomy for Ken'ichi and the others? While able to get by and keep their bellies fed, everything around them appeared chaotic and devoid of youth, with every college student scrambling to find a job…Even in these precious days of youth—once gone, never to return—everyone was being secretive and getting into confrontations.

Sakiko didn't know how many more years she would be able to live in this summer house on the beach, but she felt an acute pain and sorrow for having been born into this world.

"Can I come in?"

"Who is it?"

"It's me…"

"Sure, come in…"

Ken'ichi strolled into the sunroom, his contented expression evidence of having gotten a full night's sleep.

"Looks like you got a good tan."

"Doesn't my back have a nice color to it?"

Ken'ichi gazed at Sakiko's back, eyes narrowed as if staring at a dazzling object. It was plump, like freshly baked bread. Even the perfectly formed line of her spine made her look healthy. The skin on her shoulders seemed thin, like that of a child, and a beam of brilliant sunlight shone down onto her well-defined left shoulder. Beyond the window was the ocean, glittering in the afternoon sun.

"Ken'ichi, when are you coming back to Tokyo?"

"Hmm…maybe in around a week. I'm not heading out until the end of February or the beginning of March, so for the time being I'll be coming back fairly often…"

"You don't have to do that."

"Why do you say that?"

"Just because…you can do whatever you want, and you're feeling satisfied with your future all worked out, right? Me, I'm just waiting here to die. You don't need to come to see me…"

"You've been acting strange these days. Why have you gotten so pessimistic?"

"How rude of you, I'm not pessimistic at all…"

Sakiko got up out of the rattan chair and wiped her chest and arms with a dry towel. Her breasts were tiny, like those of a young girl. Ken'ichi wiped her back with another towel from the desk.

"Katsuko really put on weight, didn't she?"

Ken'ichi said nothing.

"I don't mind talking about Katsuko today. After all, you're all like strangers to me now…"

Sakiko put on her orange blouse and spoke as she did the buttons across her chest, one by one. "What happened to Sakurauchi and the others?"

"A little while earlier she went with Nakahori and the handyman to go see the seine fishing nets…"

"Oh really…That Sakurauchi is such a strong-willed girl…I think working at an iron manufacturing plant in Yawata is a perfect fit for her. Everyone is going to graduate college, get a job, find a wife without falling in love, have children, and live happily ever after, right?"

"Alright, that's enough…Saki, inside your head you're imagining all sorts of things, giving punishments and rewards to people as you desire…I think maybe that, in the end, the most natural way for us to spend our days is just living an ordinary life…You know, I think you've been reading far too many books. You're ill, and you must overcome your illness. For the time being I think it's best for you to live a carefree life, spending each day sunbathing, taking walks, and eating delicious food. But when you get irritated, everyone around you does too. Yesterday, you brought in all that sand, remember? I like the innocent Saki much better…and I think simply getting a job, getting married, and living out one's days peacefully is more than enough…"

"Oh, how dreadful! I can't stand close-minded young people like you with your dried-up adolescence…"

"Dried-up adolescence? I don't think I'd call it that. Adolescence doesn't have to be a succession of dramatic events. It depends on your situation—the adolescence of a noble, the adolescence of a peasant, even the adolescence of company workers like us. The lives of the characters in your novels are only stories created by the author. Can't you get rid of your preconceptions that say our lives in the real world have to be a certain way? It's possible to maintain a sense of youth throughout one's life, and I'm content with merely getting a job like everyone else, and making my parents proud of me…"

Sakiko kept quiet.

"According to you, Saki, youth is supposed to be about neglecting one's duties and loving a woman with all your heart. But even that is, in the end, nothing special…"

Ken'ichi went to open a window, and gazed out at the sea for a while.

As he watched, the sea gradually became a brighter shade of blue. In the sky, white clouds floated by.

"Ken'ichi, you can only say that because you have a long life ahead of you. But I...I don't even know how long I'm going to live..."

"What are you talking about? I just said you can't give in to your illness...You're still young, so if you just get a little more rest you'll put on some healthy weight just like your sister Katsuko did..."

Ken'ichi couldn't help but pity Sakiko, still young and living on this lonesome coast as she battled her illness.

Ken'ichi was a distant relative of Sakiko's family and stayed in their house after entering Waseda University. He was in love with Sakiko's older sister Katsuko, and wanted to marry her after he graduated college and got a job.

However, one day Katsuko unexpectedly married into the family of a simple merchant as part of a commonplace marriage arrangement.

For a time he was in a state of shock, as if a prized possession had been stolen from before his eyes. But Ken'ichi eventually recovered and even managed to return to a well-ordered life.

Before Ken'ichi knew it, Sakiko had become acutely sensitive to his affection and faint yearning for Katsuko. But it seemed that this sensitivity tended to make her distort the truth and overthink things, even to the point of being unhealthy.

Ken'ichi, seeing Sakiko grow quiet after his comment about needing to put on weight like Katsuko, sighed and immediately regretted saying that.

"In the near future I'll come back to Chiba once or twice. I still have a lot of interesting things to talk about with you. Despite what you think, nothing dramatic happened with Katsuko and I, and I'm incapable of any such drastic behavior. As you know, Saki, Katsuko is an extremely reliable, yet simple person, but at this point, if I could, I would like to make you my wife. But I'm not at the liberty to abandon my career in order to be at your side constantly...Eventually, when you recover from your illness you should come to Manchuria to visit me…You see, sometimes a man must abandon a cherished romance for his career, and I don't mean just for financial gain…No matter how wonderful of a romance I have, I'll probably end up going to Changchun anyway, and beginning a fresh, new career is the most important thing to me in my life now…"

Sakiko said nothing. The bright sunlight shone down upon the entire tatami floor, projecting an abnormally large hunchback-shaped shadow of Ken'ichi.

"I said that's enough, ok? I'll never be able to go to Changchun… I have my own life, and I'm fine with saying goodbye to you like this. After all, I'm sick…"

Getting the feeling someone was calling his name, Ken'ichi spun around and looked out the window toward the ocean. Nobeoka was standing outside the fence, his face pale.

"What's wrong?"

"Last night I stayed at the hotel in front of the train station…I'm just here to pick up my hat."

"Alright, come in then…"

Ken'ichi slid his glasses back in place and immediately went downstairs. Sakiko left her chair and went to the window, where she began to sing in a soft voice. The waves and the sky were part of the ever-changing flow of time, where all things were fleeting. Sakiko was being tormented by envy of Ken'ichi's new life, the envy only felt by a narrow-minded woman. She couldn't compel Ken'ichi to stay here with her. But did men really find a career that attractive? Sakiko had to continue living here, on this beach—plagued by her illness, she was forced to live her days here in a foul mood.

What is life, anyway? What is this "life" humans clamor about progressing towards?

Sakiko felt an unbearable pain, as if her skin was being torn open.

Sakurauchi, Nakahori, and the others returned from the sea, like mature freshwater fish heading inland. Sakiko waved a white handkerchief from the window. Both Sakurauchi and Nakahori were running fast on their way back. *Oh well, they are all moving on to their new lives…* As she waved the handkerchief, Sakiko thought about how she would be left again on this coast all alone, and felt a curious sentimentality.

"Well then, goodbye! By the way, I bought some new clogs in front of the station!"

"Oh, really? You should come to Tokyo…"

"Sure, I'll visit once more before you head off to Changchun…"

Sakiko saw Nobeoka's gray hat outside the fence. Without looking back, Nobeoka walked along the hedges, heading the opposite direction as Sakurauchi.

The sea suddenly darkened, and outside the fence a rolled-up newspaper, perhaps picked up by a passing gust of wind, blew away towards a nearby stone wall.

THE TRYST

The unheated room was chilly, so I lay in bed with Keisuke. Since we had been talking the entire day, once I slipped into bed I lay silently on my back, eyes open and hands resting on my forehead. Keisuke also pulled his hands out from under the covers. I placed my hand into his large palm. "Are you cold?" Without a word, he gripped his large hand around mine, enveloping it. The rain had continued since morning, calming me. I didn't feel like doing anything. A man whose heart sparkled like morning dew on a blade of grass, Keisuke made my heart jump with joy. We stared at the ceiling together, fingers entwined and bodies stretched out on the bed. Rain pelted hard against the window. It made a *drip, drip* sound passing through the gutter, like water falling on a rock, and the sky was a dim yellowish-brown, the air laden with moisture. The maid said that on clear days Mount Fuji was visible from the window, but last night when we arrived at this inn the rain had already begun, and there was no sign of the mountain. Apparently during the war this place served as a dormitory, and now this decrepit room had little more than a heavy mattress and a dirty tatami mat. Keisuke and I had somehow ended up all the way out here in Kofu city. This traveler's inn was the result of our search for a place with a hot spring, but neither of us minded the grimy room. I was pregnant with Keisuke's child. The peach-colored pajamas I wore were sewn baggy, for the most part hiding the unsightly form of a pregnant woman. Sometimes, as if struck by a sudden recollection, Keisuke would put his ear to my belly and listen to the sound of the child breathing within. Keisuke had a wife; I, a husband. The war had ended, but this difficult situation of ours, having no relation to the war, managed to avoid collapse. It was just that I had to begin preparing for my child to be born several months from now.

We hadn't had a proper meal for breakfast or lunch, yet neither of us felt particularly hungry. We wanted to lie together like this, even for a short while, resisting the fate that was trying to leave us behind. It felt like we were gripping each other tightly, refusing to let go. I thought that at least for this moment, god would take pity on our honest, glittering souls. I had managed to push aside those dark disturbing feelings that usually accompany trysts like this, and made peace with myself. Once in a while we told jokes and laughed. We had no time to really decide anything; nor did we have a desire to trick the world and stay together. There was an odd silence, like the enjoyment that must come to a prisoner in jail, even if only in their mind—a warm satisfaction, as if we would continue laughing together even if thrown into a valley. Believing that a happy ending would never come to two people like us, I was also comforted by the fact we were beyond the age of worrying needlessly about a dark future. I can just feel it—happiness, or at least that's what I think it is. I decided that this was enough. Is there any reason to want more? After everything that happened, is there any need to try and justify how we got into all this?

Although seemingly irrational, there was a perfect logic between Keisuke and I. A logic born from our weakness, and while nothing to brag about, we hadn't even the slightest belief in farfetched miracles. We were convinced that only after accepting that we might lose everything could we get through hard times like this.

Immorality, adultery, fraud—society would surely sling these stones at us. Even so, we could always lie together peacefully, smiles glowing on our lips. Because this was *not* a mistake. If anything, my seven years of marriage was a mistake, at least that's how I felt. The only things to judge me now were the wind and the sky.

I never considered marrying Keisuke. When the time came to part with him, I'd just have to accept it...But I had confidence that we probably wouldn't have a messy breakup. I simply wanted to raise a happy child until it began to think for itself, and then allow my child to lead the life it desired. Unlike those young girls, I didn't concern myself with the myriad distractions of the world. I just loved Keisuke dearly. My heart only had room for him. We were able to get together whenever we liked, but sometimes two months passed without seeing each other. We had faith that even if we were apart for a long time, we could meet at any time, on a moment's notice. There was no dark specter of our past towering over us. We weren't able to tease one another with words, like playing with a child's toy. Nor could we ask anything about each other's daily lives. Keisuke was a heavy smoker. I didn't smoke myself, but I always carried a match with me. That was my only way of keeping him on my mind. Sometimes when I was working in the kitchen I would light a match, and gaze at the flame for a while. Feelings of gentle affection radiated out from it, like the light of Venus slowly orbiting the Sun. Always fitting comfortably inside that flame of memory was Keisuke. Just like with the observation of celestial bodies, we are under the illusion that we completely see and understand everything there is to know about the human heart, but I feel there are many mysterious holes in our morals that leave much to be said, much to be discovered, and I refuse to believe in those morals. I refuse to believe in human knowledge that has a beginning, but like the tail of a comet has no defined end, disappearing silently into a world of nothingness.

"I wonder what time it is."

I took the hand that Keisuke still held and placed it gently against my chest, turned over onto my stomach, and grabbed the wristwatch from beside my pillow.

"It's odd we haven't been eating much."

75

"What time is it?"

"Three."

"What do you want to do?"

"I'll go take a trip to the city. Maybe I'll pick up something from there."

Keisuke got out of bed and changed. I grinned when I saw his head nearly touching the ceiling. He stepped into the hallway but returned a moment later, saying he forgot his wallet.

"You silly man."

"Yeah, but I blame you…"

"Just don't drop your wallet, OK?"

"Don't worry, I'll be fine," he said and left.

Having met as surgeon and patient, it was a little sad that we didn't have a single common friend, but now I felt that having no shared friends was a blessing in disguise. An unobtrusive general practitioner without a doctorate degree, Keisuke was a man lacking the ambition to become a great doctor. With a modest temperament that didn't try to keep up appearances, he had been loved by several women before me. I heard that after graduating from the University of Kyushu School of Medicine, Keisuke spent some time in Singapore.

But I didn't care at all about Keisuke's past. I fell in love with him naturally. At first, I had the impression he was a man with a harsh tongue, and his way of speaking angered me. Ironically, as a result I began to quietly observe him. Despite being a meticulous worker who was considerate toward his patients, he had a terribly crude way of expressing himself. For some strange reason I dreamt about him two nights in a row.

In a room of an unfamiliar hotel in a foreign land, a place deep in the mountains shrouded by mist, I dined in the light of a lamp. Beside me was Keisuke, and across from us sat two soldiers having dinner. Then, the next night I dreamt that I was searching for Keisuke's room, and the instant I gently opened his door he yelled out, "Who's there?" There was nothing particularly special about those dreams, but they haunted me for a long time after that. Whenever I met Keisuke in reality, his tongue was as sharp as ever. At the age of 34, three years younger than me, he was in the prime of his life. During the war Keisuke had his own practice in Aoyama, but when his house was destroyed in an air raid he forced his family to evacuate to their hometown of Himeji, staying in Tokyo by himself to work in the operating room of a certain hospital. I always used to joke how his chloroform anesthetic worked like a charm, and that was the only time the normally sharp-tongued Keisuke would blush, a hint of a grin on his face.

Soon after getting together we discovered that our past experiences held surprisingly little power over us, and this brought us great joy, as if we both had suddenly been born out of thin air. I thought that the mystery of Adam and Eve represented a love like ours. I have an old memory of once seeing the amorous Leda embracing Venus in my father's study and being in shock for some time afterwards; at times, I daydreamed that Keisuke's hands were the wings of Leda. To me, passion is like a sea overflowing with water.

My husband knew what was going on. He didn't say anything, but his behavior clearly indicated he knew. Even so, he never asked who the other guy was. And I didn't want to talk about Keisuke. My husband was growing old and had worked a regular schedule as a bank employee for the last twenty years. He told me that after the war, there were a few people with a fortune of one hundred million yen, one in Tokyo and three in Osaka, as well as a certain wealthy person with six billion yen who inquired about starting a bank. There was angry talk about how recovering from inflation required repeatedly putting a halt on the issuance of new currency, and how the plan to incentivize deposits with gifts was proof that we could no longer trust the government.

My husband's personality was the farthest thing from a life of ambition and opportunities, and to me his life was nothing more than a bronze statue.

Around thirty minutes later Keisuke returned with eggs, sausages, and a roll of bread. The hem of his pants was soaking wet. One look at the eggs and I felt nauseous. I touched my hand to my forehead; it was a bit warm. Keisuke popped a pink Estriol pill into my mouth.

"Your face is pale."

"Yeah, it seems like it's swollen."

Taking a sip of lukewarm tea, Keisuke took a distasteful bite of the bread. As I watched him eating, our slowly degenerating relationship brought to mind the setting sun, glowing and even somehow innocent.

I got up and sat before the dressing table.

My pudgy waist looked awkward. My legs cramped up, my belly suddenly seemed to be sinking downwards, and for a little while I was unable to move.

"What's wrong?"

"My leg muscles hurt."

"It's probably because you stood up so fast."

"Maybe I angered the gods?" I joked. My legs hurt so bad I nearly broke out laughing. Keisuke silently stared at the ground.

"I really think we should perform the operation soon."

"Operation" referred to the act of us formally moving in together. Tears welled up in my eyes. I felt pity for his wife, whom I had never even met, and some place deep inside my head began to throb.

"We don't know what will happen until it happens. When the time comes, I'm sure things will work out somehow. I think trying to plan our future together in secret is unfair to both of our families. Let's just leave things to fate, I don't think there's any other way. Rather than trying to figure out a solution to all this, I'd like to just have this child as soon as possible. To me, all the effort required to give birth is going to be far more difficult than trying to solve our problems. I don't care about the 'operation' at all…"

"But if you don't give birth at home, what are you going to do?"

"I'll just go out to some city and have the child there. There's this clinic I found."

Around a month ago, I headed through sleet and rain to visit a tiny maternity clinic in Zoshigaya that I heard about from a newspaper advertisement. The cheerful midwife treated me as if she understood everything and said I had nothing to worry about. If I intended to give away the child, then there would definitely be someone to receive it, so I should relax and come back when the time was right. I had no intention of giving the child away permanently. I simply thought that if a kind person was available, it would be acceptable to place the child in foster care for the time being. After sitting in the dim room for a while, eventually a married couple entered who said they wanted a child. As is often the case for a place where a woman spends all her time working, this room was dusty and cluttered, and the chubby midwife smoked vigorously. They had apparently come for a pre-arranged appointment because a young girl came down from the second floor carrying a baby wrapped in a red hemp cloth with a leaf motif.

"Fate works in strange ways. This is going to make this baby very happy."

The middle-aged couple took turns cuddling the child and staring at its face. It was heartbreaking to watch them act like they were judging the quality of some product, and I couldn't bear to sit there any longer. No matter what happened, I never wanted to put my child through something like that. A little while later an envelope of money was handed over and the couple left carrying the child and a large box. The young mother immediately returned to the second floor, a dejected expression on her face.

"You see, it all works out surprisingly easy."

The midwife lit a cigarette at the electric stove, as if relieved by the completion of a job. When I had her show me the second floor, there were three people surrounding the girl from a moment ago, whispering softly to one another. Each mattress in the room was worn out like an old rag, and a pungent odor tickled my nose, perhaps because the shoji doors were shut tight.

Magazines littered the floor, pages splayed open in disarray. There was a pair of tiny baby beds. The first was apparently the bed of the baby that was just adopted; beside that was an aged trunk whose lid was left open.

In the other bed rested a light-skinned baby of indeterminate gender, eyes wide open, that must have been around two months old.

When I thought how I too would be laying here four or five months from now, a vacant feeling came over me.

However, when I realized this might be the last place I saw alive, I felt a certain yearning for even that dirty delivery room. But I simply wouldn't stand for Keisuke coming to see the child. I could just imagine how terrible it would be to witness the dejection of a man feeling sorry for the fate of a woman giving birth in an unfamiliar place like this. I simply couldn't expect a miracle or anything like that in this world. The only guarantee in life was that each action comes with a consequence. At this point I didn't think it was a good idea to pity or be lenient on myself. Considered as adultery according to the morality of this world, our love was undoubtedly seen as an indecent thing, an object of despise...

I just couldn't bear to expose myself to that sort of hatred.

I think that upon seeing a person's downfall, what can be considered thoughtless misconduct, a surprising number of us would secretly harbor feelings of spiteful delight. For I have seen countless people watching someone suffering in a pit of despair and yet make no effort to toss them a lifeline, only criticize as they please...

"It doesn't look like the rain is going to let up any time soon."

"I wish it would rain forever..."

"Don't say careless things like that."

"Did I say something wrong?"

"You sure did..."

"It's just that sometimes I get irritated like this."

"It'll be August or September, right?"

"You mean my due date?"

"Yeah."

"Honey, when the time comes, will you come see me at the clinic?"

"Of course I will."

"Oh really...but maybe it's better that you didn't...because I feel so bad for you..."

"But it's better if I went with you, right?"

"That's true. It would be nice if you came..."

When the time comes to go to the clinic, I'll have to take care of a bunch of things. It's depressing to think about how it's always the woman who ends up with the short end of the stick, having to deal with everything by herself in an awkward situation like this.

Something terrible is approaching us day by day, and yet we never talk about it. It's because we're fully aware that having a discussion about the future a few months from now won't change anything...But more than Keisuke, it's me who is clinging tightly to the desperate hope that we don't make things end tragically.

"Don't you want to try a sausage?"

"No, I'm full. But I would like to drink some hot tea with pickled plums."

Keisuke drooped his head again in silence.

A stray lock of hair on his forehead gave Keisuke a certain youthfulness. I took out a package of seedless plums from my travel bag and popped three in my mouth. They left a sour, refreshing aftertaste on my tongue.

"You really have it rough..."

"Huh? What do you mean?"

"I just mean that it must be hard on your body...but there's no way around it since you believe the impossible is possible. Nevertheless, time marches on, and you manage to stay surprisingly confident and determined—you're hopeless."

"Well then, what do you think we should do?"

"Two people in love should be together...There's no other way. If that is going to make someone suffer, then the sooner the better, right?"

"Yes…but, I can't help worrying about so many things, and becoming discouraged by them. Will you promise me you won't get upset when you hear this? Sometimes, I just wish I could kill you. I'm hopelessly in love with you, so I don't want to cause any sorrow to you or your family, even the tiniest bit. This is *our* problem and nobody else's, and it horrifies me just to think about making people unhappy who are innocent bystanders. But I know it's not fair of me. The way I'm thinking about all this is probably based on these really, really old traditions. It might be unfair to say this, but ultimately it's only our problem. And that problem is…well, you see it pains me just to imagine making other people suffer for our sake."

"How selfish of you."

"I'm not so sure about that…I don't know how to explain how I feel, but ultimately it's just too much trouble for me to make others suffer— although I guess maybe things will work out in the end…Anyway you don't have to worry about all this. The only thing we can do is let things run their course, and hope everything will work out…"

Even though it was already April it was still cold in the outskirts of Kofu, perhaps due to the rain, bringing a chill to my fingertips.

"Let's take a bath."

"Yeah, it's gotten a little chilly."

Keisuke and I went down a long hallway and entered the hot water. In the afternoon bathhouse there wasn't a single person bathing.

After undressing, my blue-veined, bloated belly made me uncomfortable. I was weighed down by this great feeling of repulsion, like when you see something ugly. Trying to avoid looking at each other's bodies, Keisuke and I entered the water a distance apart. A pleasant mist filled the bathhouse.

"Don't I look like a racoon dog?"

"What?"

As if surprised by my remark, Keisuke, who had been washing his feet, suddenly turned to look at me through the steam.

"I feel kind of like I'm a racoon dog. I thought that was really funny…"

"Honey you're losing your mind, little by little. You're coming up with these nasty thoughts on your own and irritating yourself."

Keisuke looked down again and started rubbing his feet. I heard the sound of an airplane, like the rumble of distant thunder, but it suddenly became a deafening roar, so close that I thought the plane was coming crashing down onto the roof of the bathhouse. Something black, like a monster in the form of an airplane, flew by with a great sound, blocking out the windows of the building.

Someone even rushed outside in the middle of the storm to see what happened.

"Hey, isn't that airplane going to crash? I wonder if it's going to be alright, do you think anyone can save it? I'm sure it's going to crash at any moment. Come on, you really have to save that airplane! No! No! It's so terrible, out there in the rain like that…Hey, don't you think anyone can do anything to save it?"

I frantically opened a window and gripped it tightly as I stared at the airplane roaring away into the distance, screaming Keisuke's name at the top of my lungs.

"It's going to be fine. That was an American airplane. They're built quite sturdily so it's not going to crash."

"I don't believe that. Even American airplanes can crash. I really feel bad for the person inside, maybe someone can save them…"

Keisuke put his shoulder around me as I tightly gripped the window.

"You're going to catch a cold, Mrs. Crazy Woman…Alright, let's get back in the water. I'm starting to get a chill. Look, those airplanes just don't crash very often."

"That must have been the sound of the plane falling down. Once, a long time ago, I saw an airplane crash back in the countryside…."

"Don't worry about it. You're being silly…"

Keisuke wrapped my waist with a towel. "Well now, this mother and child are a little heavy," he said, lifting up my freezing body with ease and carrying me into the hot water. As if trying to blow away the steam, a southern wind suddenly blew in from the window I'd hurriedly opened a few moments ago. It seemed like someone just flipped on the power switch because the light inside the dome ceiling's glazed window turned on.

"You're just like a child. When you get in the water, your body swells up."

"But it's so strange that even if a plane is about to crash, nobody is able to save it…"

I held Keisuke's hands and gently spun around in the water of the wide bath. When I tried to suppress the anguish caused by my jumbled mind, abnormal thoughts began to surface. A strange fear that the domed roof was going to fall down right on top of me struck my body like a shudder. I felt the baby stick out its legs, sensing the warmth of the bath water. There was a pain in my belly, a sensation of being pushed. This tiny thing, tied to me by fate, began to moan with its head facing down…To me this lonesome baby, quiet and content without bothering anyone, was unbearably precious. I decided I would have the baby in that clinic, in peace. I just wanted to give birth quietly, without troubling anyone.

If I could only give birth to a healthy child, I wouldn't need Keisuke. Sometimes, when we got a chance, him and I would meet at a train station in Shibuya. We would wander through the remains of the burnt city, never speaking a word. And whenever we came to a certain place upon a small hill with a magnificent view, we would sit upon a mound of burnt rubble and gaze down at the bustling city market.

Having gotten out of the water first, Keisuke waited a while for me to get dressed.

"See? There's nobody making a fuss about an airplane crash…"

"The pilot must have done a good job landing…"

"I told you, those things don't crash easily."

We returned to the room to find an early dinner tray prepared for us. Upon the tray was a truly pitiful meal. The rain continued to fall in a light drizzle. We decided to stay one more night. Smiles spontaneously appeared on our faces, as if we had been permitted to live an additional day. But within our smiles was no particular sentiment. While we ate at the oddly shaped table, for the first time I felt uneasy about being away from home for two nights in a row, and resolved to tell my husband everything when I went home tomorrow. The waves crashed and dissipated—water splashing to a distant place from which it would never return.

Like a great flood we all walk together, pushing and shoving each other...I am in that crowd too, trying to frantically keep up with uncertain steps. Countless faces emerge, each burdened with countless worries. I have no choice but to continue pushing my way forward in a daze. Even if my entire life is destroyed for the sake of this love, I will regret nothing.

Obscured by the rain, Mount Fuji was not visible the entire day. But I knew that the moment the sky cleared, a massive mountain would appear before my eyes. As I looked out from the second floor, within the twilight mist a verdant, green cornfield stretched far into the distance.

DAYS AND NIGHTS

All things in life, even breakups, are the natural result of a series of events— so agreed Kakichi and Nakako as they laughed out loud together. But while something deep in Kakichi's heart refused to call this "natural", Nakako on the other hand felt a modicum of relief, as if savoring the loneliness of becoming a single woman. Then, as if acknowledging that their bout of oddly timed laughter meant things were actually over, Kakichi picked up the teapot, refilled their cups and said, "Well, since you're a fairly carefree woman I doubt you'll worry like I will, but I hope you'll at least take the time to keep in touch," placing each cup onto the edge of the brazier with a *clink*.

"You're *still* talking about that? Even after we break up, if one day things improve for both of us then we can get back together again. You shouldn't say sentimental stuff like that, it will only bring us down..."

" 'Bring us down'? That's funny, considering it was you who suggested we split up."

Nakako said nothing. Just a moment ago they were enjoying a laugh together, but then Kakichi turned all mushy, which only served to further irritate Nakako. Kakichi was lying on the floor, looking around the room as if nothing had happened, when he glanced over at Nakako's nonchalant expression and thought, "This is the woman I've been married to for a whole four years," feeling a fondness towards even the fine lines on her forehead, like the attachment one feels for a well-worn tool.

"Well, whatever...I just mean we should properly take care of ourselves."

"My goodness, we haven't even said we are breaking up for sure, so it's strange for you to say something like that."

Now it was Kakichi's turn to be sullen as he realized the unexpected lack of emotion in Nakako's demeanor. "We might actually be breaking up this time," he thought and lowered his head onto the tatami mat, squeezing his eyes tightly closed.

"Hey, what's wrong? Is the light too bright?"

Kakichi didn't answer.

Seeing Kakichi grimacing with his eyes shut, Nakako thought perhaps the light was too bright for him and pulled the netted hanger to move the light above his head into the corner of the room. After standing up, she sat down at the dresser and dabbed some honey on her pinky, then applied it to her chapped lips. It wasn't like either of them had any particularly great memories, and as she stared into the dresser's mirror, Nakako felt chills, as if soaked by the spray from several years of braving rocky seas with him. But at this point she wasn't motivated to continue this kind of life with him, and while it might seem cold-hearted, she had long ago grown tired of Kakichi's personality. "Even if we do break up, I wish things were like in the old days when we could do whatever we wanted. But with things as they are, without even a cent to my name, it makes me sick to my stomach to know I won't be able to provide any support for you." When the topic of separating came up, Kakichi said things like this to pretend he was a nice guy and didn't give Nakako a chance to respond. But it embarrassed her to hear him say that, since even when things were going great for Kakichi she didn't particularly enjoy her life, and was surprised she had been able to hold out four years living what was, to her, an utterly primitive life being supported by a man like him. Kakichi frequently talked about how they could do whatever they want in the old days, but he only had a men's clothing shop in an isolated building that didn't appear to be particularly successful, and to a stylish woman like Nakako who moved in with Kakichi shortly after his previous wife's death, it seemed like a dismal lifestyle. Whenever she sat at the dresser his ex-wife had used, Nakako couldn't help but feel an eerily pale ghost staring back at her—a ghost by the name of "Tsuru." When Kakichi was 32 and his ex-wife Tsuru was 29, they had opened a tiny men's clothing shop inside a strawmaker's building in Kagurazaka, but it was a north-facing place away from the street with only about 25 square meters of space, and for the first winter Nakako was bedridden with chronic anxiety, probably due to the lack of sunlight.

Despite being called a men's clothing store, there was little actually sold except for inexpensive goods used by college students, like shirts and accessories such as socks, whereas the hunting caps and white long-sleeved shirts of poplin cotton sat untouched like ornaments on the shelves for the entire four years, gathering dust as their colors faded— no matter how little sunlight there seemed to be.

"Hey Nakako, come here for a minute. I want to tell you our store code."

Only a single day had passed since Nakako moved in with Kakichi. After closing up shop early, there were various goods on the table beside the register—boxes of scarves, shirts, and handkerchiefs—and Kakichi explained that their code was "Tsu-ru-ma-hi-o-ri-ta-yo-shi-se-maru," which she should memorize. He quickly explained to Nakako, who wasn't very familiar with math, about the meanings of the various amounts, where "tsu" corresponded to "1", and each subsequent letter to the next number. For example, "o-ru" would be 52 sen, and "tsu-ma" would be 13 sen.

"This code represents the cost we obtained the item at, so you have to mark up each item ten or twenty percent for us to turn a profit. For that customer earlier, I often forget to use the code and sell it for the wrong price, so make sure you don't rush when checking people out."

For the next few days, Kakichi nagged Nakako persistently about the code, but she eventually got upset and complained about how she detested the code, and how tiresome it was to keep using something like that. When Kakichi thought about it, he realized that the code was indeed too suggestive, having been made from the letters of his ex-wife Tsuru's name and the meaning of the first character of his name. But as he was watching Nakako pouting and getting angry, there suddenly seemed something cute about her. So, thinking it would be easier for both the seller and the buyer, he decided to put on proper prices like they did in the department stores, and rushed out to buy a rubber stamp that he used to stamp prices over top of the codes. However, for a woman like Nakako who was accustomed to a carefree life, she found it terribly bothersome to say things like "These underpants will come to sixty sen" or "This is a high-quality shirt made of elastic material, and we do not consider it expensive at a price of only one yen and 20 sen." Each time there was a sale that involved something like a customer paying a cost of one yen and 89 sen using a ten-yen bill, she would come rushing into the back of the store and tell Kakichi to do it. In the beginning he thought this was funny, but even after two or three years Nakako never even tried to get used to the store work, instead finding a sunny place where she would open up a book to read some heroic war story, and then when summer came around it was her that was bothered by the heat more than anyone else, laying out a straw mat on the kitchen floor and rolling around on it like a fish. There were times when Kakichi thought he was burdened with this terrible woman, but Nakako was oddly skilled at doing kitchen work while acting like it was nothing at all, and Kakichi would unexpectedly find one or two of his favorite dishes prepared on the table at mealtime. On days when they had made money, sometimes he even found a bottle of warmed saké upon the brazier. To tell the truth, Nakako was more of a saké-lover than Kakichi, and he frequently chastised her for gulping down cold saké in the kitchen. But she would say, "It's not *me* that likes saké, it's my stomach, so there isn't much I can do about it," and when getting drunk at night she would always slip into bed and dramatically moan, "There's a ghost! There's a ghost!" But she neither saw a real ghost, nor did her conscience conjure up an imaginary one as a form of punishment; she was simply just not comfortable drinking alcohol and saying, "Oh my, I feel terribly giddy," in front of her husband, so she would instead yell, "There's a ghost!" and shake her husband's pillow box to unsettle him, while in her mind she felt wonderful and imagined sticking out her tongue like a cow. Being who he was, whenever Kakichi heard "There's a ghost" coming from the adjacent bed, a faint chill ran down his back, but he would think she was probably embarrassed and so decided to remain quiet, letting her say whatever she wanted. But when Kakichi kept quiet, Nakako would ask "So, are you scared?" and the next moment became silent herself like a little child, only to suddenly feel a shiver running down her spine, wondering if he used to sleep like this with his deceased wife, and then she would say, "Hey, wake up!" as she tugged on his pillow. Whenever this happened, he would fall into his usual habit, no longer able to fake being asleep; for some strange reason he never got tired of this woman. In bed Nakako would calmly talk about how she thought about other guys, as if she was a woman of loose morals, but unlike his ex-wife, she didn't feign innocence and sleep with other people, and Nakako was at heart a girl who had worked in a small restaurant, so besides being unreserved she didn't talk about *that* subject as if it were as tasteless as the rainy season, like an ordinary wife would have done, and with Kakichi she always behaved like a playful, wild mountain beast. As he ran the duster across his socks and shirt boxes, Kakichi would sometimes idly wonder where she got all that energy from.

Around the time of Nakako's second year living with Kakichi, the stock on the store's shelves drastically dwindled, as if a well had gone dry, their goods becoming insufficient to the degree that whenever a half-dozen of anything was ordered, like a handkerchief, they had to make an embarrassing refusal as the liveliness visibly disappeared from Kakichi's demeanor. A businessman at heart, he had not received any assistance when opening this store, so when there was a great reduction in stock—essentially his self-earned fortune—there wasn't anyone to reproach him, although both Kakichi and Nakako somehow felt that the end of the line was that much nearer.

"Kakichi, do you think maybe I should try working at that other store again?"

Sometimes, on the way home from the grocer or the public bathhouse, Nakako would look at the job postings for restaurant waitresses and reminisce about when she used to work in a place like that, thinking that if she had the chance, maybe she should try to get a job as a waitress again—as if starting work would make the money start immediately rolling in.

"You shouldn't say stupid things like that. Just think about your age. A woman's career in a place like that ends in her early 20s...You're already 27, do you think you're still a young girl?"

Hearing this, she would refute him by saying, "Since I've never given birth to a child, I'm basically a young woman anyway," and pass the days with a definite, though submissive insolence. But each time they got together, the topic of breaking up would arise for some reason, and when those arguments continued late in the night, before they knew it morning had come, and they ended up opening their shop later than everyone else in the area, even losing out on a little business.

In early summer of the third year of their marriage, when Nakako finally took their sole bicycle and sold it, their store was bare like the display floor of a thrift shop, with only a few empty knitwear boxes set cleanly aside that strangely testified to how bad business at the shop really was.

Despite being a coward, Kakichi was rather obstinate, and this part of his personality persisted even after she moved in. But once he started taking responsibility for a woman like Nakako, the business that he had seemed to maintain when married to his previous wife now felt uninteresting, like a shop selling cheap goods, and he found himself trying his hand at the markets. Starting from a place of very little capital, he unknowingly got involved with a certain swindler, lost everything, and even tried to get into horse racing. But in the end Kakichi decided to try a high-interest lender he had heard about in the newspaper, and ran back and forth searching wide-eyed for a small credit firm. But like sinking in quicksand, the more he struggled the more he got pulled down, and all of his possessions disappeared one by one, leaving the store deserted. Once he had nothing left to stock the shelves, Kakichi went to a makeup wholesaler near Asakusa and purchased some cheap pomade and liquid facial powder, and put a few items on the shelves, although this was ultimately little more than a show of vanity and over a year's worth of rent went unpaid; after everything that happened he owed so much money that the landlord's wife came crying to the entrance of his store.

Putting honey on her lips and licking them carefully with her tongue, Nakako stood up suddenly, as if remembering something, and then pulled a padded kimono robe from the closet, placing it on Kakichi's knees. After the topic of breaking up had been broached by his woman, Kakichi was stuck in a loop of dark thoughts, eyes shut tight, as he considered himself to be the worst possible man.

"But about what we were talking about…it would be better for both of us, right? You should completely forget about this store. To begin with, anyone purchasing a handkerchief would want to get it at a department store, not to mention even if somebody were to give a few thousand yen to a small store like this, we wouldn't be able to survive."

"Yeah, you're right. Lately department stores have been springing up all over, and since anybody can open a place like a market with a bit of money, nobody will pay any attention to a gloomy store like ours…The times have changed, and even if someone gives us a few thousand yen, I'm finished with this business."

"Then what will you do?"

"What will I do? Well, first I need money, no matter what I'm going to. Without money, nothing will get done…"

"That's true."

"And well..."

"If you get rid of all the furniture and other junk, about how much can you make?"

"We owe the landlady rent so we probably shouldn't sell the furniture. If we sold the other junk cheaply somewhere, at most we would get enough to stay one night at a hot spring..."

"Hot spring? That sounds nice. It's sad, the cherry blossoms are almost finished blooming, but we haven't done anything special..."

Nakako remembered her days standing all day while working at a restaurant five or six years ago, when her legs were numb at the cherry blossom viewing parties. On the other hand, whenever Kakichi heard the sound of the chilly wind outside, he felt like having some saké.

"By the way, isn't it going to be April in a few days?"

"If I say yes, you're just going to say you wish we weren't together anymore, right?"

"I'll leave that up to your imagination."

Just then Kakichi stood up suddenly, making the robe fly off as if he had kicked it, took a gulp of the cold tea, and said, "Now that we've settled on breaking up, let's head out to a hot spring somewhere."

After stewing in her depression for the last few minutes, when she heard Kakichi suggest going to a hot spring her eyes sparkled brightly like a little girl, and she cried out "Oh my!" with an alluring voice. Rather than trying to go day-by-day and stretching things out tediously, it would be better to just quickly sell everything off and head to a hot spring, and it wouldn't be too late to break up after that, in fact it might make for a cleaner break that way, thought Nakako. "That sounds wonderful! Just think about it, there's no point to standing here worrying about things," she said, hurriedly grabbing a ledger from the store and opening it in front of Kakichi.

"Try writing down in this blank area what we have and how much we can sell it for."

"You mean the market price of our junk?"

"There's a bunch of stuff left like the register and display boxes, right?"

"Yeah, those are there, but I put all of them up for collateral on my loans…"

"Collateral? When do you go off and do such a thing?"

"When? Oh, that was quite a long time ago. Honey, we don't have a single thing to our name."

Nakako didn't know Kakichi had gone as far as doing things like that to cover his debts.

"In that case, we'll have to leave late at night, since in the light of day we can't sell anything."

"That's true."

"Oh dear, it's not like we've been wasting money or anything. Compared to the markets and horse races, this tiny place isn't worth anything. Not to mention that you made high-interest loans without telling me. You shouldn't have done that…"

Even so, Nakako was happy to visit a hot spring with Kakichi. She couldn't wait to sell off each and every item in the store and then jump on a steam train. "Hey, let's make this work out. We at least deserve a few good memories out of all this," she said and gazed up at the light in the corner of the room, squinting against the brightness.

The next day, to avoid attracting attention they called in a passing elderly junk dealer and cheaply sold off everything from bedding to kitchen utensils. It was a beautiful day with particularly dry air, and the road in front of the strawmaker was peaceful as always. Bucket in hand, Nakako made little splashes as she walked nervously back and forth on the gutter, like a person cleaning the sidewalk, hoping the landlady or the wholesaler clerk didn't show up before the junk dealer returned. Once the dealer was done making several trips carrying various odds and ends away, Nakako smiled vacantly as she exchanged glances with Kakichi in an empty room inside.

"How much did you sell it all for?"

"Ru-ta-yo-maru."

"Oh, well…27 yen and 80 sen, we almost made it to 30 yen."

"We should be glad he bought this much from us…"

They sold even the dresser and the brazier. Unsurprisingly, the drawers used to carry everything were huge themselves, so they sold those too, but Nakako couldn't shake the feeling that Kakichi regretted selling them. Once evening fell, they put on as many clothes as they could, squeezed the rest in a tiny trunk, and locked the front door sometime in early evening before heading outside, deliberately together. "Ah, that's a relief!" said Nakako, feeling cheerful as if about to head home to her parents, but a bitter taste remained in Kakichi's chest. As Kakichi began to think about the store, so tiny and yet serving as the place they had lived and worked for the last six years until today, he felt a faint warmth in the back of his nose. When they started out on the road, he casually turned around and saw the store's sign, lit by the glow of twilight, seemingly beckoning him to enter. An inexplicable sense of desolation flashed through Kakichi's mind: after bidding farewell to this store and to this woman, where was he supposed to go? Where was he supposed to live?

The Kagurazaka streets were chilly and covered in dust, but the city lights were bright and the crowd plentiful, imparting a certain energy to the air.

"Kakichi, it looks like Koyama increased his stock again. He carries knitwear with that sheep logo, but with a rent fifteen percent above our store, how does he manage to be so profitable?"

"It's obviously because of capital. If we were able to increase our stock, or open up a Mitsumame sweets store, then things would start turning around for us too."

When they passed by a Koyama western goods store—where a suited salesman stood smoking absent-mindedly with a head of hair glistening like the eyes of a dragonfly, and inside a case covered by a roughly six-meter single pane of glass were displayed canes, fedoras, and stylish Swiss-made sport shirts—they involuntarily stopped in front of the window. But to them, it was nothing more than a nostalgic indulgence; there was nothing inside that left a particularly vivid impression on them.

Kakichi and Nakako wandered aimlessly through the dusty city towards Shinjuku.

"I want to buy a toothbrush."

Because Kakichi said he wanted to buy a toothbrush, the couple made their way through the crowd and into a department store. It was the kind of place that was open late, with lighting so bright it would give you a headache and fake cherry blossom branches decorated around the store. While sifting through an assortment of cheap toothbrushes in the makeup section, Kakichi caught sight of Nakako quietly slipping a round case of lipstick into the darkness below a shelf. Wishing he hadn't just seen that, he hurriedly paid and then led Nakako out the back door of the store. Kakichi acted like nothing had happened, but in truth some part of him felt that they had just taken revenge on countless department stores. Nakako herself seemed indifferent, later asking how many years it had been since they rode a steam train, or saying that the reddish moon was pretty when they were viewing the cherry blossoms, even though the dust was terrible.

They left that night on a steam train to Atami.

The inn they stayed at was tiny, located within a residential area far inland. Opening the window of their room revealed a giant, hazy moon. Having never traveled with a woman like this before, Kakichi felt like a teenager again and drank more than Nakako. "Who cares about that stupid store anyway. I'm going to make even more money and surprise you," he said in unusually high spirits, patting Nakako vigorously on the shoulder. But whenever Kakichi began talking about the store they left behind, Nakako was seized by an image of his late wife's ashes flying through the sky, making an eerie rattling noise. A portion of her ashes had been sent to her hometown, where they now rested in a small urn on the household altar. Every time Nakako heard Kakichi belittle their old store, she grimaced at him, wondering if he too was thinking about his ex-wife's ashes.

Once the alcohol took effect, Kakichi wept loudly on Nakako's lap like a little child, saying things such as "If I only had 500 yen..." and "How is breaking up going to help anything?"

They stayed two nights at Atami.

The warm weather made their coats unnecessary, and buds were freshly sprouting from the apricot trees on the shady side of a mountain. While staring absent-mindedly at the apricot grove upon the bank, they periodically saw a steam train rush by above the trees. Gazing at this scene, the idea came into Nakako's head of ending her life together with Kakichi, yet that was only a passing fancy, and like an elongated earthworm, she eventually found a warm spot of sunlight and relaxed with a war chronicle book rented from the inn.

"Well, I guess it's almost time to go back to Tokyo..."

Nakako remained silent, staring at him with a stern look as she wondered how long he was going to mope around and draw things out. Then they got back onto a night train. Despite traveling together for two nights, there hadn't been any particular revelations, only the noncommittal atmosphere of breaking up that endlessly tormented them. As for Nakako, when she tried thinking about the situation realistically she remembered how old she was, and how weak her body had become. She was unable to believe that after splitting up with Kakichi, her life would immediately make a turn for the better. And for Kakichi, if he just had enough money he wouldn't particularly regret losing a wife or two, but after getting rid of the store, not to mention losing all his money, the idea of separating from his wife and living on his own seemed unbearably lonely. He had literally nobody but himself, and while the idea of building a life seemed like a heroic thing when his wife had been around, as a man in his late 30s an unspeakably desolate feeling towered over him, saying this was all a futile display of power, and that emptiness gripped Kakichi's heart with great force. How much easier it would be to simply die of starvation with his wife.

Once they returned to Tokyo, as they had discussed on the train the couple decided to visit a few restaurants on the backstreets of Shinjuku in search of a waitress job opening. For the time being, Kakichi said he would help find a place where Nakako could settle down, and then go off to wherever he pleased.

"Kakichi, it looks like rain."

"Yeah, it's going to rain a little."

Kakichi straightened the collar of his sun-bleached Inverness down coat and gazed up into the sky. Despite being the one to suggest breaking up, after everything that happened Nakako must be feeling lonely too, thought Kakichi, and if she wasn't able to find a job he was prepared to stay at a cheap inn on a side street somewhere. When they came upon a street in the back of Shinjuku with a row of cafes, pork cutlet shops, and other restaurants, Nakako handed Kakichi a cloth-wrapped parcel and proceeded to go into each restaurant that looked promising. In the end they had success with a tiny rope-curtained bar, but the moment she left the building Nakako came running back to Kakichi with a look of embarrassment.

"Don't worry, this is just for now. It's good temporary work. And it seems like a friendly place, don't you think?"

After managing to reassure Nakako, Kakichi handed her the parcel, with the message behind his words crystal clear: *After walking around like this, I guess you finally realized how old you really are.*

"Alright, let's exchange our addresses once we figure them out. Although I'm probably going to have to go walking all over the place for the next few days...Anyway, take care of yourself..."

With this, Kakichi lifted up the trunk that had been resting on the gravel, but Nakako walked beside him for a few steps as she said, "This is my share of the money we just divvied up, but I want you to have it," grabbing up all the coins from her handbag and quickly pressing them into his hand.

Just then it began to rain, large drops glittering on the eaves of each building. "Just go. You'd better hurry up and get to work so you can clear your head." About ready to take off running, Kakichi was surprised to see the heavy rain and hid under the eaves of a gas station, but when he glanced at his black shadow stretching out onto the rain-soaked sidewalk, the stark hopelessness of his life struck him hard.

"Are you OK?"

"I'm fine."

Standing under the gas station's eaves, they both felt like bursting out laughing, just as they had back in their store in the strawmaker's building. But Nakako made up her mind and stepped out from under the eaves. No matter how much time they spent there was no end to this, and if things were eventually going to turn out this way it was better to just make a clean break now and go where she pleased. This went through Nakako's mind as she entered the rope-curtained building whose wooden sign read "Koiso," and she never looked back. Inside on the dirt floor was a customer sitting with a woman, poking at a pot while drinking saké. When Nakako reached the front desk the head hostess, breastfeeding a baby, led her to a tiny tatami room in the back. "Put your stuff here, and then come out to the front," she said. The second floor was only around four meters long, where a few customers were singing and tapping their bowls. There were only two waitresses, hair tied back in *marumage* style, wearing stylish imitation striped *omeshi* kimonos or something similar; despite being a tiny rope-curtained restaurant, this place wasn't too shabby.

Although exhausted, Nakako donned a simple checkered silk crepe kimono and a belt made of two types of plain *habutae* silk woven together. The waitresses glanced at Nakako's clothes and casually grumbled, "Sadly, we're not very busy."

As soon as Nakako left, Kakichi began to feel like an honest-to-goodness traveler, struggling to carry the old trunk as he threaded under the eaves, gradually heading towards Shibuya. The rain let up,

99

and once the foam on the ground dried up the dust-smelling sidewalks glistened with water, as if a sprinkler truck had just passed through. Kakichi stopped in front of a western goods store several times. Hunting caps, neckties, pajamas, white long-sleeved shirts—various items spiraled around and around in his eyes. Each time he came to one of these stores he would pause. He thought that next he would try returning to the store in Kagurazaka. While he couldn't go back to living there, he wanted to at least see from afar how his old place was doing, but it was already pretty late at night. When he came across the sign of a merchant inn that said "Iwataya Inn," he shoved the glass door open with his shoulder and entered with unsteady steps. As a girl with black earlobes served him tea, looking as if she just came in from the mountains, Kakichi absent-mindedly wished that this misery would be the first and the last time in his life. If he knew loneliness as intimately as his own hand, then it was like countless of the same gaunt hands were now grabbing at him from all directions. He was unbearably lonely. Kakichi gulped down the rest of his tea and began thinking about how Nakako, penniless, was serving drinks to strangers in a place not very far away, when all sorts of absurd thoughts rushed into his head, like how he should have stayed another night at Atami with her. After he asked the housekeeper to lay out his futon he felt a burning, decidedly unmanly sensation behind his eyelids. He hadn't been able to express it in speech or writing, but after separating from Nakako, his love for her came cascading down like a waterfall, and an undefinable fear drifted through not a stream of difficulties with money or life, but through a torrent of love for a tiny woman, and the next moment Nakako's name was on his lips, about to be spoken.

A suburban train rushed by down below the window. Before he knew it, Kakichi was snoring loudly, sound asleep with the light above still on.

For Nakako, something bothered her about how they ended things, and despite being utterly sick of Kakichi's personality, she couldn't sleep well in her room when she thought about how he had gone off somewhere, drenched, in search of a place to work. She even considered how Kakichi, being a coward, probably wouldn't commit suicide. Maybe he had returned to the strawmaker's place and was sleeping there as if nothing happened, thought Nakako, disturbed more by how far she had fallen than by Kakichi's cowardly behavior. If she was going to feel this terribly lonely, then maybe it would have been better to stay in their old store and try to somehow eke out a living. But when she thought about the Koyama western goods shop that attracted customers by selling the popular Mitsumame sweets, and the other western goods shops of various sizes packed together in that neighborhood, it seemed as if all these stores were struggling desperately, just like Kakichi and her had been.

She just couldn't bring herself to put it on in front of Kakichi, but now that Nakako looked at the lipstick stolen from the department store under the light it seemed surprisingly gaudy, and this annoyed her, made her wonder what was going to happen to her life, and even when she tried laying down getting any sleep was hopeless.

The following evening, Kakichi came to visit her, bringing neither his coat nor his trunk. Nakako was happy to see him, but she pursed her lips in a show of annoyance as she pulled him under the restaurant's sign.

"So how was it? Do you think things will work out here?"

"It's not a very nice place…"

"That's what I feared…"

"Where did you stay last night?"

"Last night? Oh, I ended up in a merchant inn."

"Really? You didn't try to go back to our old store?"

"Are you crazy? I can't go back there. If they found out, we could be in real trouble."

"So did you decide anything?"

"Well, I didn't really decide much, but this morning I went to

Asakusa, and if I wanted to open a night stall to sell makeup there is this place which will let you borrow a few products for consignment sale, so I was thinking maybe I should try that…"

Even though the topic of breaking up had arisen countless times during their four years together, once they finally separated—whether a result of their absolute poverty, or some lingering attachment stemming from their age—it felt good to both of them to get together like this, even if some loneliness remained.

"A night stall?"

"That's right. What do you think?"

"Well…a night stall might be nice, but lately there are department stores all over the place, and things aren't like they used to be. The pace of life is faster too…So what kind of stuff do you want to sell?"

"You mean what products?"

"Yeah."

"Lemon toner, polishing oil, whitening powder, stuff like that. They say I should be able to buy one bottle for *tsu-o* [15 sen] and sell it for *ma-o* [35 sen], so if I can get 24 bottles in one day I should be able to easily make four yen, right?"

"Well, that's how it is supposed to work. It depends on the area, but I actually think that it would be more profitable to go around to villages in the country and sell department store clearance goods, or something like that. Running a night stall in Tokyo…even an amateur like me knows that isn't going to work."

"Yeah, well I agree a night stall probably won't work, but these days just traveling around the countryside is pretty expensive."

"Not to mention that if you open a night stall in Tokyo, you'll have to worry about the rain and wind. And four yen a day? If it was possible to make just 120 yen in a month, we wouldn't hear horror stories of night stall merchants hanging themselves. What do you think will happen when the rainy season arrives? Then business will really dry up."

"Alright, but you don't have to be so serious about it. This is just the beginning…By the way, what do you think of opening a stationery store?"

"Hmm, maybe that's better than selling makeup."

They had stepped out from under the restaurant sign and started walking a little. Both Kakichi and Nakako were excited about the idea of opening a night stall. As they walked, sometimes Nakako would express her annoyance when Kakichi seemed to be hopeless without her around, but she would also sigh and remark, "You say that after breaking up during these bad times you feel horrible, but after everything that has happened, now I feel like I'm the miserable one. I can't even look myself in the mirror." Kakichi felt a strange sensation in his body, unsure if he was actually alive, or whether his legs were wandering around on their own accord. Although he had brought up the idea of opening a night stall, even consignment sales required capital. All they claimed was that putting down ten yen of security money would allow borrowing products valuing a little above that, and the prospect Kakichi mentioned of making four yen in a day was indeed probably nothing but a fairy tale.

"Do you want to head over to the inn for a little while?"

After seeing Kakichi's ragged form, Nakako couldn't turn down his offer. When they entered the inn, a person at the desk stared intently at the coatless Nakako as if Kakichi had just picked up a girl off the street.

In the room was a cold, warped square brazier, a lusterless desk littered with graffiti, and Kakichi's trunk that sat orderly beside the desk. Neither of them could decide quite where to sit. Nakako opened a window, purposefully making a loud rattling noise, and sat on the windowsill. Below, a brown-colored suburban train passed by.

"You slept here?"

"Yeah."

"This room is pretty empty, huh."

"It's just a merchant inn, what did you expect?"

After standing there vacantly for a while, Kakichi laid down near Nakako and smiled. "It sure would be nice to have some saké."

"Kakichi, your hair has grown awfully long. You should go to the barber."

"Well, I'd like to go to the barber, but more importantly, I can't settle down in a place like this."

"Yeah, women can settle down anywhere, but for a man it's difficult when you get in a situation like this."

As Kakichi gazed at Nakako, whose choice of words had been particularly cold, he realized that Nakako seemed much more like his wife when she was stealing that lipstick. Just judging from the formality of her speech, some distance had already grown between them, so Kakichi shook her leg and whispered, "Come here."

"Stop it!" she said, brushing his hand roughly off like an eagle cleaning its feathers, then stood up from beside the surprised Kakichi.

"Are you really going home?"

"Yes, there isn't much purpose in staying here like this!"

Kakichi said nothing.

"Hey, what should I do now? By the way, what did you do with your coat?"

"I sold it!"

"Yeah, I guess that's OK since it's gotten warmer, but before you lose every shred of clothing you have to do something, whether it be that night stall or something else."

"Don't tell me what to do!"

"What…did I say something to upset you?"

"How can I not get upset? I'm not in a daze like you are, no, I'm thinking about so many things it makes my head hurt! If we split up now, you'll be able to live an easy life, right? Because nobody ever gets tired of a woman…That's all marriage is anyway, if things go sour you just bid sayonara and go your separate ways…"

Kakichi was quickly getting lost in a world of his own words.

"I don't believe you're going off and saying something like that again…especially after we had such a nice talk and agreed this was all just for the time being, until things get better…But I guess you'd be happier anyway finding a much better wife than me, and having a child…"

Kakichi stood up, quickly grabbed her chest, and pushed her down to the floor. Through the open window Nakako caught a glimpse of a hot air balloon spinning high in the sky.

The slap to the face burned, but Nakako refused to cry. She closed her eyes and remained silent. Kakichi sat astride her, breathing heavily, but once his hands went slack on her neck they both fell silent, and at that moment each of them suddenly remembered how Nakako had always used to say, "It's a ghost! It's a ghost!"

Something wild and violent remained in Kakichi's heart, but he had already come to his senses.

"Are you alright? I'm so sorry!" Kakichi said, gently embracing her neck and lifting her up.

"After this, I can't even call myself a man anymore."

Nakako said nothing.

"You should fix your belt, and hurry back to the restaurant."

Kakichi stuck his head out the window and ran his hands through his bushy hair like a madman to try and shake out the dust. Lying down, Nakako stared vacantly at the hot air balloon floating in the sky outside. She wouldn't likely ever find another man who would seriously hit her after breaking up, but she *really* wouldn't find another man who would lift her gently back up after doing such a thing. More than the suffocating feeling in her chest, it was the loneliness she felt when gazing at that balloon—like a full moon at midday—that made her about to break out in tears.

"Kakichi, you know what? I don't intend to go back there again!"

Kakichi was speechless.

"I'm staying with you. Even if we try to break up, if we don't wait until things get better with our lives, we'll be haunting each other forever, like ghosts."

Nakako got up and sat beside the silent Kakichi on the windowsill. Facing downwards, her husband was ruffling his hand through his hair, scattering dust on the train tracks below, and into that gaunt hand she placed her tiny comb. "Oh, this is nice," he mumbled, grabbing the tiny, ornate comb, and began pulling it against his scalp with an audible scraping sound.

Nakako stared one-by-one at each speck of dust scattered across Kakichi's tired shoulders, deciding it was best to leave tomorrow for tomorrow.

BEYOND HAPPINESS

Kinuko first met Shin'ichi in a cramped second-floor laundromat where the windows let in the rays of the setting sun.

It was an unusually warm December day, making the charcoal heater unnecessary. Shin'ichi wiped his forehead frequently with a handkerchief.

Now and then Kinuko looked over to observe Shin'ichi's expression.

Framed by two large earlobes, his face was pale from a long hospital stay and yet showed no signs of worry. Shin'ichi had a square jaw, but Kinuko detected a certain familiarity in his face—occasionally looking toward the wall as if to avoid the rays of the glaring sun—almost like she had known him for ages.

Shin'ichi sat beside a window, clean-cut in his suit. Yoshio, serving as a matchmaker, clumsily carried over tea and sushi, his head bouncing from side to side.

"Kinuko, please offer some sushi to Shin'ichi," he said, heading back downstairs as if to attend to some business there.

A fly flew above the sushi, tiny wings making a dull buzzing sound. Swatting it away, Kinuko quietly approached the plate of sushi, serving some onto a small dish which she rested on Shin'ichi's lap. He blushed, picking up the plate with both hands. Kinuko snapped apart a pair of wooden chopsticks and placed them wordlessly into Shin'ichi's hand, which he quickly raised above his eyes in a sign of polite gratitude.

When her finger made contact with his for an instant, Kinuko felt a warmth constricting her chest.

She was quite fond of Shin'ichi.

Strong feelings of affection overflowed from deep within her, the kind of feelings with no logical explanation.

Shin'ichi remained quiet, the plate resting on his lap.

A beer company's tall smokestack was visible outside through the glass door. The silence made Kinuko uneasy, so she poured a few drops of soy sauce onto the dish, then carefully put some on each piece of his sushi, one at a time.

"Oh, thank you..."

Shin'ichi lowered his gaze slightly when he caught a whiff of the soy sauce, blushing again in embarrassment. Kinuko thought Shin'ichi was a good man, and she should start a good conversation with him. So she ran various ideas through her mind, but couldn't settle on a topic.

Shin'ichi had on lightly tinted glasses that gave the impression of a man in good health without eyesight problems.

She mustered up all her courage and asked, "So Mr. Murai, what do you like?"

"What do I like? If you mean food, I'll eat anything."

"Is that so...But what is your favorite thing to eat?"

"Well, my favorite thing is...I guess I like udon..."

"Oh, really," said Kinuko with a giggle. She herself loved udon, and when she lived in the Ninomiya household the daughter there also liked it, so Kinuko had prepared lightly seasoned udon nearly every day.

At the word "udon" Kinuko suddenly heard the clear sound of waves crashing at the Omaezaki coast, as if they were in arm's reach. Kinuko and Shin'ichi shared the same hometown, and he was 28, seven years apart from her. Shin'ichi had returned last year from the war with only one eye.

**

Less than a week after a brief first date as part of the arranged marriage, they held their wedding ceremony. The couple got a place to live near the train station of Chikusa City. Soon after settling down in their new home, they asked Yoshio to watch the house while they returned to their hometown of Omaezaki.

Shin'ichi's family was poor, living off a mix of fishing and farming, but his father and his older brother's family were all good people. Apparently, Shin'ichi's mother died when he was very young.

"You see, my family was poor," he told Kinuko one evening. "So my dream was to become a rich, prominent man after I graduated middle school...but I couldn't continue to afford middle school, dropped out partway through, and became a potter at a ceramics company in Nagoya. Later, I went off to war and came back with only one eye...I think of this as a kind of fate, and I guess you could say escaping with my life was a special sort of fate, as was my marrying you..."

Shin'ichi lowered his gaze to the warm kotatsu table where they sat, as if reminiscing about events from long ago. He could hear the gentle shushing of the waves.

Shin'ichi's parents' home was crowded with a large family, so they had rented Kinuko and him a single room in a neighborhood tea house adjacent to a lighthouse. There they spent their days freely, without concern for others.

When night fell, the lighthouse would cast a yellow beam across the distant sea. At times, the sparkling light would waver above the dark ocean like the stalks of a wheat field waving in the wind. The lighthouse's light shone beautifully on rainy evenings, too.

Soon after graduating from her village's middle school, Kinuko traveled to Nagoya, where with the help of Yoshio, a relative, she became a live-in maid for the Ninomiya cotton wholesaler family.

As an attendant to the family's daughter, Kinuko spent her days until age 21 without any hardship. But this spring the daughter got married and left for Tokyo, and so Kinuko moved out of the Ninomiya household and went to live at Yoshio's place.

Kinuko was not a particularly beautiful woman, but she had a certain charm, likable thanks to an ample figure and easygoing personality. While at the Ninomiya house she received two marriage proposals and was forced to meet one of the suitors, but she didn't like the man. A knitted-goods merchant, he had apparently already had his share of fooling around, and even with Kinuko he made lewd remarks from the start, bearing yellow teeth as he smoked incessantly.

She found the man unpleasant and promptly declined the marriage proposal.

Kinuko couldn't help but hate all this—did marriage really have to be such a superficial thing? But at the same time, there were days when she succumbed to a terrible pain, a burning heat that racked her body.

When Yoshio first mentioned Shin'ichi, it was fair to say that she honestly wasn't very interested. After a bad experience she had grown tired of meeting suitors, and Kinuko wasn't very fond of merchants or craftsmen. Her dream was to marry someone who worked for a large company, but even so there was something attractive about a man who returned from the war with only one eye, so she decided to give him a chance.

Kinuko felt he was a good man when they first met, but once they got married she discovered him to be a truly compassionate person.

She couldn't help laughing to herself whenever Shin'ichi woke up in the morning singing at the top of his lungs.

He would sing every morning without fail, and only the kinds of songs that children liked.

***

After lunch, they walked once more down the concrete steps beside the lighthouse and on toward the beach. It was a cold day, but the wind was calm, and the surroundings peaceful. Out in the ocean, shrimp boats were casting their nets.

A net was laid out to dry upon the gently rolling sand. Shin'ichi and Kinuko sat on the beach, leaning against the wall of a straw hut used to store the nets. It was quiet all around, so they could feel the sound of the waves in the pit of their stomach. The gentle breeze blowing across the gray ocean smelled of salt, a scent somehow reminiscent of medicine.

"Let's take a few deep breaths of this air before we head home," said Kinuko, speaking as a child would.

Shin'ichi remained quiet for a while, perhaps listening to the sound of the waves, but then raised an eyebrow and turned towards Kinuko, as if suddenly remembering something.

"Shall I light you a cigarette?"

Unwrapping the handkerchief and removing the cigarettes and matches within, Kinuko placed a cigarette on Shin'ichi's lap.

"You know, there is something I've been meaning to ask you. What did Yoshio tell you about me?"

"About you?"

"I mean about my past..."

"What about your past?"

"It seems like Yoshio didn't tell you much about my past in order to protect me..."

"What was I supposed to ask him about? Why should I care about your past anymore?"

"Well, it's unfortunate if you haven't been told yet..."

Wondering what this might be about, Kinuko struck the match. The blue flame was hot on her fingertip. Shin'ichi took a slow puff of tobacco, savoring the taste. The white smoke drifted over towards the sea and quickly dissipated.

"I wonder if Yoshio told you about my child."

"What..." Kinuko caught her breath, staring into Shin'ichi's eyes.

"Just as I thought. Yoshio didn't tell you about that, did he?"

Shin'ichi stood up without another word and began slowly walking alone to the water's edge. Kinuko stared at him for a while, but couldn't help feeling that Shin'ichi wasn't telling the truth. And yet, come to mention it, in his room there had been a photograph of a child. Was it on the desk, or on the wall? Perhaps she hadn't paid much attention to that picture because she never thought he had been married before. The picture of a child that she had glimpsed seemed to be a girl.

Kinuko wanted to hurry after Shin'ichi, but for some reason felt it was best to leave him alone.

That man has a child? Kinuko just couldn't believe it. With his padded kimono coat, inverness cape, and walking stick, Shin'ichi's figure wavered back and forth unsteadily.

Wrapping up the matches and cigarettes back in the handkerchief, Kinuko stood up and walked towards Shin'ichi with uncertain steps. He was whistling quietly.

"I really don't like seeing you walk away by yourself like that..."

At the straw hut it didn't seem particularly cold, but once she started walking towards the shore a chilly wind blew by that nearly made her gasp.

"You'll catch a cold, so let's go back," Kinuko said softly, grabbing the sleeve of Shin'ichi's coat.

With no one else around, the desolate beach was like a desert. On a hill that rose near the coast, the white lighthouse stood out in stark contrast to the cloudy sky. Even assuming Shin'ichi did have a child, why should that matter?

His sleeve still held by Kinuko, Shin'ichi returned obediently to the straw hut.

***

When he was 22, Shin'ichi went to Nagoya and was employed as an office worker for a ceramics company. Manufacturing ceramics for export, it was an extremely busy company, but after working for only a year he managed to accrue a small savings, so he returned to his hometown and found a wife. She was a petite, talkative girl, but soon after giving birth to their child she ran off to Manchuria with one of Shin'ichi's friends, leaving the child behind.

After his wife deserted him, Shin'ichi was left with the responsibility of raising a child on his own. As soon as he woke up in the morning he had to care for the child and leave it with someone in the neighborhood before commuting to work; after work, he had to pick up his child. This routine continued for nearly a year. Shin'ichi couldn't help but love his child dearly. After reading a newspaper article that said children raised on only milk tended to have a weak constitution he boiled carrots and spinach, strained them, and mixed them with milk. At times, he would even grind up dried fish vigorously with a mortar and mix them with milk to feed his child. The child grew up surprisingly fast, earning the nickname "Mr. Murai's wondrous child" around the neighborhood.

Shin'ichi had to take care of everything himself, from changing diapers to mending clothes. Fortunately, the child never needed to see the doctor, even once. Even if it had stomach problems, as soon as Shin'ichi came home and cared for the child, it would regain health.

By the time he had to go to war his child was already crawling, but because Shin'ichi knew this time he should not leave the child with a neighbor, he decided to give it up for adoption before heading to battle.

When he gave the child up for adoption, Shin'ichi thought that this might be the last time he saw his child. Even if he returned home with his life, he felt that the child would not survive that long. Shin'ichi was sending his child to a place where even providing milk and porridge would be difficult, but unlike a child growing up on a traditional diet his child had to be fed strained carrots, spinach, and apples. So he withdrew his entire savings and gave it to cover the child's expenses. Shin'ichi did consider leaving the child in Omaezaki, but since his brother already had four children he decided to send it instead to live with a different family.

After three years Shin'ichi returned from the war to find his child still healthy and strong. But when he went to visit it, the child had trouble warming up to him, frightened by Shin'ichi's black eyeglasses. At the foster home, the child was cared for like one of their own, which is probably why the woman there burst into tears, saying it was heartbreaking to be asked to return the child.

Even after marrying Kinuko, Shin'ichi was unable to forget about his child. The more he tried to forget, the more he remembered the difficult times spent alone with the child. Despite remembering nothing about his ex-wife, Shin'ichi still longed dearly for his lost child to the point of shedding tears even in his dreams.

He would buy carrots and boil them late at night while playing with the child. A healthy child that never cried, even when left alone on the tatami mat the child would move its lips and babble as it played there.

Shin'ichi would strain the boiled carrots, mixing them into the milk to make a thick texture. And when he placed a bottle of the mixture near the baby, it would kick its cute little feet in delight.

Sipping at saké beside his giggling baby was Shin'ichi's most beloved pastime. He would sprinkle soy sauce on the leftover boiled carrots and eat them as a side dish while drinking.

After heading out to war, whenever Shin'ichi looked at a picture of the child he would break out into sobs from unbearable sadness. He yearned deeply to see his child, feelings so intense they would be considered unmanly. Once, in a particularly fierce battle when the bright yellow blossoms of the apricot trees were in bloom, he was watching the enemies' movements out the window of an elementary school building. *You shouldn't stand up now, it's dangerous! Daddy, I told you it's dangerous!* He could see the soft fingers of his child's hand reaching towards him vividly in mid-air. He should have completely forgotten all about his baby on the battlefield, but for some reason he saw the image of his baby clearly in the midst of bullets flying about.

Shin'ichi fired without restrain.

He brought his face up close to the window and fired round after round, brushing away the child's hand before his eyes, when he suddenly heard a deafening bang right above his head, and felt a sensation like his face was being gashed open with a thick blade.

His body felt like it was sinking into a deep, dark hole.

The cries of his baby continued ringing in his ears, and he began to lose consciousness.

The child's gentle voice resonated up from deep in the ground, like a whirlpool. Lured by the voice, Shin'ichi fell faster and faster into the bowels of the earth.

When Shin'ichi returned to a hospital in his hometown, his ex-wife—supposedly in Manchuria—showed up unexpectedly. Infuriated at the woman, Shin'ichi was unable to speak. When he remained silent, before leaving she asked where their child was. Shin'ichi no longer had any feelings for the woman, but when the matter of his child came up he found himself growing angry again.

***

"In the teachings of Buddha, it is said, 'Earthly desires are unending, yet we must vow to sever them from ourselves,' but no matter what I do, I cannot sever my desire for this child…I asked Yoshio several times to tell you about my child, and to ask you to only come see me if it didn't bother you…When I came back injured, everyone only pitied my physical appearance and tried to keep me happy for the moment, hiding the truth—but I thought doing that would lead to an unhappy future for both of us…and yet I know that, having already married you, it's too late to do anything about this…but still, in the beginning of our marriage I wanted to tell you about this once more, this time coming from me. I did think that maybe Yoshio never actually told you…but I guess I was somehow scared and wanted to be with you no matter what…You might laugh when you hear this, but these are the genuine feelings of a man…That time you put soy sauce on my sushi, I was incredibly happy. The smell of the soy sauce brought back so many memories that it nearly made me cry…"

Then, as if relieved of some great burden, Shin'ichi released the sand held in his hand, now warm and damp, and let it fall upon his knees.

Kinuko had a vision of a large group of dark-colored birds swooping down onto the sea. *My husband once had a wife, and a child…* The first night she arrived at Shin'ichi's house, Kinuko remembered him talking covertly with his brother about something…and now she felt her future becoming darker by the moment.

For a long time, Kinuko gazed far across the sea.

Living together with a child on the second floor of someone's house, feeding it only carrots and spinach…Kinuko could not detect even a hint of those forlorn days in the Shin'ichi who stood before her.

"You know…"

"What is it?"

There was something warm and welcoming in Shin'ichi's words. Kinuko didn't know how to handle this. Perhaps because she had worked as a maid in a respectable, well-to-do family since she was 16 years old, Kinuko now had the sensation of suddenly falling into a great pit of misery.

"How old is your child?"

"Already four. She can even sing."

"So you want to see her again, right?"

"Yeah…"

"I guess the mother lives around here?"

"I have no idea where she is now…But I don't give a damn…"

"But don't you…"

"I hope you aren't regretting marrying me…"

Kinuko was silent. She opened up the handkerchief gently and took out the cigarettes and matches again. But just as Kinuko withdrew a chalk-shaped cigarette from a box labeled "Hikari" and slipped it between Shin'ichi's lips, his warm hand suddenly grabbed her fingers and he began to bite her fingernails, one at a time—pointer finger, middle finger, ring finger, and pinky.

Kinuko swallowed hard to try and keep back the overflowing tears.

***

For the first time in a week, the couple departed Omaezaki and returned to Nagoya.

Despite being in the midst of a war, the city in near twilight looked busy as ever.

Their new residence was on the end of a row of four townhouses, the scent of fresh wood hanging in the air of the newly built building. Tatami mats with a soft core were used, but still made a creaking sound.

Like a couple who've spent many years together, they felt at ease with each other and shared whatever was on their mind.

Shin'ichi got a position at the ceramics company he used to work at years ago; he worked each day spinning the potter's wheel, relying on the blurry eyesight of a single eye.

When they notified the Ninomiya family that Kinuko had gotten married, the daughter, now in Tokyo, sent a beautiful vanity as a wedding gift. There was a letter attached:

Kinu, I can't imagine a person more fortunate than you. After getting married myself, I've experienced hardships many hundred times worse than when I was living at home. I can never return to that life, but I long terribly for those days.

The daughter was a young, pretty woman, but according to a store clerk the man she married was quite a depraved character, causing her much distress.

The upper floor had a single room of ten square meters, and

downstairs there were three rooms of ten, eight, and five square meters. There was also a little bathtub, and a garden where chrysanthemums bloomed despite the small area.

The Chikusa station was close by, and the prices of goods in this area were relatively inexpensive.

Kinuko was thinking of going to see Shin'ichi's child by herself. The fact that he had been quiet about this lately made Kinuko that much more keenly aware of his sorrow, and the memory of that day on the Omaezaki beach was still vivid in her mind.

The child had been left in the care of a family running a grocery store named "Ōsone."

When Kinuko told Shin'ichi that she was planning to go to Ōsone alone to visit his child, Shin'ichi said he wanted to go with her, and so one Sunday in the early evening they took a train to Ōsone. Their train car was relatively empty, but across from them sat a family with three children. The oldest child, seemingly a middle-schooler, wore an overcoat with gold buttons down the front. The second oldest was probably in sixth grade, and the youngest in second. The three children sat between their parents, talking about their visit to Atsuta Shrine. The father, aged around 45 or 46, had fallen asleep with arms crossed, a camera hanging down loosely from his shoulders. The mother was a large, portly woman, leaning backwards against the window with legs apart. At times she would scold the children for hanging on the train's leather straps, and the children would frequently put their hand on the mother's neck, pestering her about something later in their trip. Kinuko felt a tickling sensation like sweat dripping down her back. Could Shin'ichi and her live a happy life like that family?

Staring out the window, Shin'ichi was beginning to doze off himself.

Kinuko enjoyed herself watching the family across from her.

Eyes closed, the sleeping father withdrew a tissue from his pocket and blew his nose noisily. After that he politely wiped his nose and, eyes still shut, lowered the tissue to his lap, when his chubby wife suddenly thrust out her large arm over the children's legs, grabbed the tissue and put it in her sleeve.

Kinuko smiled with flushed cheeks, feeling shy as if she was the one being observed. After passing the tissue to his wife, the man dangled his hands onto his lap and fell back asleep. Watching the scenery rush by outside the windows, the children laughed and joked around. Legs still open, the chubby woman exhibited a certain calmness, just as you would expect from the mother of these children.

Kinuko suddenly turned her head to face Shin'ichi. Right as the train passed through a particularly bright area, she gazed at the somehow pitiful, unpretentious form of her husband and realized that, like this woman across from her, she must be strong and protect her husband as long as she can. Not just for her husband's sake, but as a form of harsh revenge on the woman who had abandoned him.

When Kinuko thought how someday she too would give birth to several children and be able to sit like that with legs apart, she felt something warm stir within. The woman didn't look even the least bit indecent—on the contrary, she exhibited a sense of dependability as the mother of three. Kinuko tried gently removing her wooden clogs and reclining like the woman, but at her young age this felt somehow odd. About to break out laughing, Kinuko nudged Shin'ichi with her elbow a few times. But Shin'ichi, completely unaware of what was happening, simply stared out the window, a faint smile on his lips as if laughing quietly to himself.

ABOUT THE AUTHOR

Hayashi Fumiko was born in 1903 in Shimonoseki City, Yamaguchi Prefecture, Japan. Her first notable literary work was *Hōrōki* ("Diary of a Vagabond"), an autobiographical novel describing her life of extreme poverty, first published in a literary magazine in segments between 1928 and 1930. Several of her other early works were also autobiographical, but she eventually began writing short stories and novels that were less autobiographical, as well as poems, children's stories, and travelogues.

Her works were heavily influenced by the aftermath of World War II, and *Ukigumo* ("Floating Clouds") is one of her most popular, a story about a woman's struggles in post-war Japan. It was made into a movie by director Mikio Naruse that received critical acclaim in Japan and abroad.

Many of her stories focus on urban working-class life, a genre sometimes referred to as proletarian literature. Some important topics touched upon in her stories are free will, marriage, illegitimacy (she herself was an illegitimate child), and other feminist themes. Many of her stories feature strong, free-spirited women, but male characters also play an important part, sometimes serving as the main character.

Hayashi Fumiko died in 1951 from a heart attack at age 47; the previous day she had been working on an article for "Shufu no Tomo" ("Housewife's Friend"), a women's magazine that ran between 1917 and 2008, and her death is considered to be caused by overwork. Her former residence in Tokyo has been converted to the Hayashi Fumiko Memorial Hall, a museum honoring her work and the work of her husband Tezuka Masaharu, a painter who never gained significant popularity.

She produced over 200 books in her lifetime and has been called twentieth-century Japan's most important woman writer.

www.ingramcontent.com/pod-product-compliance
Lightning Source LLC
Chambersburg PA
CBHW030540130626
46552CB00006B/2352